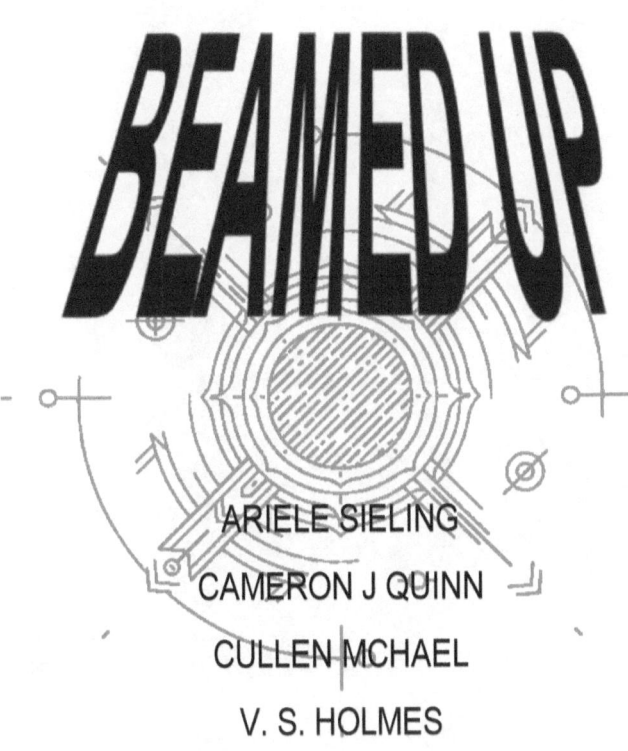

BEAMED UP

ARIELE SIELING

CAMERON J QUINN

CULLEN MCHAEL

V. S. HOLMES

AMPHIBIAN PRESS

This is a work of fiction. All of the characters, organizations, and events portrayed in these works are either products of the author's imagination or are used fictitiously.

BEAMED UP

Copyright © 2018 by Sara Voorhis

Amphibian Press LLC
P. O. Box 190
West Peterborough, NH
03468

www.amphibianpressbooks.com

ISBN :   9780998333267

Printed in the U. S. A.

Table of Contents

The Stalk

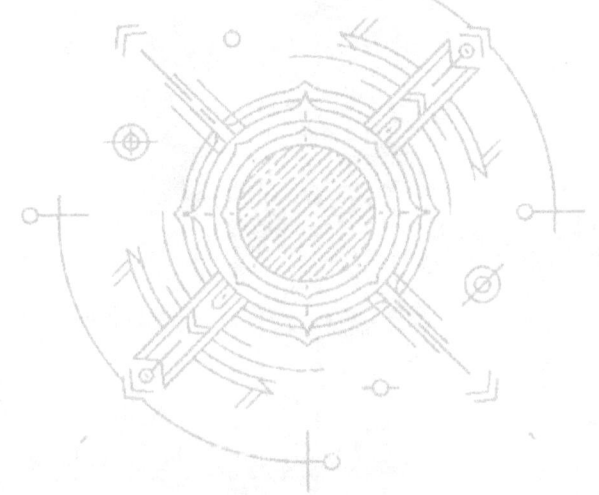

ARIELE SIELING

ARIELE SIELING

The Stalk

Ariele Sieling is the author of the Sagittan Chronicles, a science fiction series, and the children's book series, Rutherford the Unicorn Sheep, and has had a variety of science fiction and fantasy short stories published in several anthologies. She lives in New Hampshire with her husband and three cats.

She can be found at her website and on Facebook, Goodreads, and Twitter.

www.arielesieling.com

The Stalk

ARIELE SIELING

Jack stood at the edge of the Hole with nothing but a guard rail between her and a vast chasm of emptiness. She heaved a bag of dirt up and emptied it over the edge; it poured out like a waterfall, each clump getting smaller and smaller until she couldn't see it any more. Then she dropped the plastic in after it, watching the white float away, down into endless blackness the Hole.

Sighing, she wiped the sweat off her brow and turned to grab another bag, letting out a startled shriek as the holographic form of a woman wearing a tightly fitting skirt and blouse appeared in front of her.

"Do you need the perfect gift for your child, spouse, parent, or friend?" it asked too cheerfully. "Consider buying a four-foot replica of the Stalk, a gorgeous, majestic reminder of the technology that brings life to the loyal citizens here on Jord!"

"Go away, dammit!" Jack growled, mumbling her deactivation code. "B1143." The hologram winked out of existence as she turned toward the foreman's platform. "Boss! That's the fifth holo today!"

"One of the dampeners is broken," Faith yelled back. "You're just going to have to deal with it! Get back to work!"

Jack glanced at the time and then smiled. She only had ten minutes left—though, if another holo appeared proclaiming the wonders of the Stalk before she got out, she might just jump into the Hole like so many other Diggers before her had.

She tossed four more bags of dirt into the Hole, not for the first time wishing they could just use hover carts like everyone else in town. Unfortunately, the dampeners did more than just block out the stupid holos—they also made it impossible to use any hover technology within a fifty-foot radius of the Hole. Her watch beeped, and she headed toward the locker room. Faith was waiting for her inside, wearing high heels and enormous gold earrings with red LED-beads in the center.

"We'll have the holos sorted out before you get back," Faith said, looking down at her clipboard.

"What do you mean, 'by the time I get back'?" Jack asked, a feeling of dread growing in the pit of her stomach. She spun around to look at her locker; three green bulbs glowed just over the door. Three beans. That meant...

"You've been selected to do a day at the Stalk," Faith said without smiling. "Remember, you're representing all of us here at the Hole. We want the funders to understand that what we do is vital work in the community, and that we love doing it."

"I don't love it," Jack said bluntly, yanking her locker open and pulling out her backpack. Her wristband beeped as her hand passed under the beans; three green lights appeared on it. If she tried to run away, they would be able to track her down and make her go to the Stalk anyway. "I dump dirt into an endless chasm of darkness for a living. What's to love about that?"

"Pretend you do or you're fired." Faith strode away, heels clicking against the tiled floor, bracelets jangling.

"Won't matter if I'm dead," Jack muttered.

Petrov burst into the locker room, followed by Shelly.

"Drinks tonight?" he asked, before skidding to a halt. He looked at Jack's locker, then at her face. "You got three beans?" he gasped.

"Three beans?" Shelly echoed.

"You know what they say," Petrov said. "Don't drink the water, don't eat anything they give you—"

"Or breathe their air if you can avoid it," Shelly interjected.

"—don't read their pamphlets, submit to any scientific testing, don't take any pills they give you—"

"Petrov!" Jack interrupted. "It's going to be fine. I'm going to be fine."

"That's what Steven said," Shelly reminded her.

"And Paulie," said Petrov.

"Yolanda," said Shelly.

"Robby, Tonk, and Meri."

"Fink and Hazel."

"It's an 80% jump rate," Petrov added.

"I'm not going to jump into the Hole," Jack said, exasperated. "I've spent years feeding that thing—I'm not going to feed myself to it too."

"They all said that." Shelly had tears in her eyes.

"You were one of my favorites." Petrov stepped forward and wrapped her in a hug, his sweaty stench filling Jack's nostrils.

"I can't believe you got picked!" Shelly wailed, throwing her arms around both of them.

"Okay, that's enough." Jack wiggled her way out from the group hug and glared at them. "I'm not going to die. I'll be back."

"That's what they all said," Petrov said with finality, shaking his head. "We'll toast to you tonight." He raised a hand in the air dramatically.

"Fine." Jack rolled her eyes and grabbed her bag. "See you all the day after tomorrow."

When Jack stepped outside the next morning, a hovercopter was silently floating in the front yard of her apartment complex. Other residents looked suspiciously at it, Jack, and the man in a stiff suit standing beside it, holding a large white sign with her name on it.

"May I see your ID?" he asked as she approached. She held out her wristband, assigned to her at birth, still glowing with three green lights.

"Welcome aboard, ma'am."

Jack climbed in. She had only ever ridden in one once, when she had shattered all the bones in her leg. That time, she hadn't really noticed anything due to the combination of excruciating pain and mind-altering pain medications. This time, she looked around her with curiosity. The hovercopter was essentially a glass sphere with four seats inside. There was a floor under the seats, and the driver, a smiling bearded gentleman in a uniform, had a panel in front of him with a monitor, switches, and two levers that he used to steer. Jack could honestly say that she had no idea how it worked. The man in the suit watched Jack climb into a seat in the back, then sat up front beside the driver.

"My name is Leroy," the bearded driver said, "and I'd like to welcome you aboard the Bubble. Have you ever flown before?"

"Once, under the influence of pain meds," Jack replied, shifting around uncomfortably in her seat.

"Ah yes, emergency hovers," he said. "Well, mine's much lighter and faster. It can be a bit nerve-wracking at first, but this is a short trip, so just hold tight."

"Yessir," Jack said, gripping the armrests firmly.

The ground dropped away beneath them as they rose up over the apartment buildings. She could see other hovercopters in the distance, most floating around the Stalk.

The Stalk was the biggest space elevator in the known colonies. It rose up in the center of the city, a gleaming, metallic symbol of the grand innovation of civilization, or so the WIA said in their pamphlets. The Watchers and Inspection Administration was very concerned that its ever-loyal citizens understood exactly how wonderful the Stalk was—life-giver, job-creator, majestic hope for the future.

Jack didn't often look at it; it was usually just a constant grey blur in her peripheral, looming over the city, the Hole, her apartment—everything she did—her whole life. It was just there, teeming with self-important people scurrying around like ants, trying to prepare it for actual vehicles to use, and she was just an unimportant speck trying to fill a ravenous Hole a few blocks away.

Viewed from the Bubble, it was enormous, massive, growing from the ground up to outer space, filling the sky with its shining silver gleam—a space elevator truly worth the loyalty and admiration of its people. As they soared overhead, the people, the houses, the cars all became insignificant dots; but the Stalk still loomed, as enormous and intimidating as ever.

"You doing okay?" Leroy asked.

Jack swallowed. She suddenly felt a little nauseous, and the sky seemed so big she was sure she was going to drown in it; a tiny little bug like her didn't belong in the sky, she belonged in a cave or a tunnel or at the bottom of the Hole, but certainly not this high above the ground with nothing to hold her up except this glass sphere—

A loud clicking sound jerked her attention back to herself where she could feel her hands gripping the armrests so tightly her knuckles turned white, while her breath came hard and fast and her stomach roiled and churned.

"Stay with me, sweetheart." Leroy was snapping his fingers repeatedly in front of her face. "It's alright, we'll be there in just a minute. Stay focused on me, you hear?"

Jack shifted her attention to his hands, which were once again on the levers. They were old hands, worn and calloused, fingernails caked with dirt and chewed to the quick. Then she looked at his beard—reddish with curls and some grey strands woven in. She began to count his beard hairs.

When she reached three-hundred and forty-seven, she suddenly realized the Bubble had stopped moving. The man in the suit was already out of the hovercopter, standing a few feet away, waiting for her to get down.

Leroy was up and out of his seat in a jiffy, helping release Jack from her safety straps and step down onto a solid floor.

"You did great for your first time!" he exclaimed. "My sister was just like you when she started flying, and not two years later she could wing one of these things like she was born in it."

Jack let out a little laugh, relief surging through her. "I don't know how you do that every day. Or your sister."

"I don't know how you walk up to that gaping, hungry Hole every day," he replied. "That thing scares the crap outta me."

"I guess you get used to it," she replied.

"That's exactly right." Leroy smiled broadly, wrinkles creasing his eyes. "You get used to it."

Jack took a deep breath to calm herself. "Your sister close by?"

"Journey City," Leroy said. "A few hundred miles away. Haven't seen her in a couple years—haven't gotten permission to travel. One of these days though!"

She looked over at where the man in the suit was waiting. He glanced at his watch and gestured for her to hurry up.

"I have to go," she said. She let go of Leroy's arm— she hadn't even realized she still had been holding onto him.

Leroy glanced at the suit and then leaned in, lowering his voice. "Now you listen to me," he said. "You are a VIP today. Don't let them push you around. If you want something, ask for it. If you have questions, ask 'em. And if you tell them you want me to take you home, come the end of the day I'll be right here. Understand?"

Jack nodded. His face was stern, gaze so intense that she could barely look at him.

"You bring up all of us?" she asked, glancing back at the suit again. "All of us VIPs?"

"Yep. 'Cept for my days off."

"Even the… the…" She was thinking of Pauline, Yolanda, Robby, Tonk, Meri, and the others, but she didn't know how to say their names.

"Them too," Leroy said. He knew who she meant. She could see it in his eyes. "And I don't want you to be another one."

"What…" Jack hesitated. "…what was different about the others? Murphy? Lisa?"

Leroy shook his head sorrowfully. "Just one thing. They never stepped through that door." He gestured to an entrance to the building just past where the suit stood.

At that moment, the suit strode over impatiently. "We have to go now. Please follow me." He gently took Jack's elbow and began guiding her away from the hoverpad.

"But… but…" Jack protested, looking back over her shoulder at Leroy.

"Remember what I told you!" he called. "Don't let them push you around!"

The door approached faster and faster. *Don't let them push you around.* She never let anybody push her around—not Petrov or Shelly. Not Faith. Not even her mom or sister. And she certainly wasn't going to let this person, who hadn't even had the courtesy to introduce himself.

"Stop," she said, just as they neared the threshold.

"How can I be of service?" the suit asked, turning toward her looking mildly annoyed.

"First," she said, trying to think fast though her heart was racing, "tell me your name."

"I am Android 2711," the suit said.

"You're an android?" Jack raised her eyebrows. She'd never seen one up close before—only rich people could afford them, and those that had them didn't go parading them about the streets much.

"Yes," it replied.

"Can I have Leroy pick me up at the end of the day?" she asked quickly, trying to stall for as long as possible. She had to figure out some way to avoid going through the door.

"I will arrange it." The android looked down at its wrist and tapped a few buttons on its wristband. "Is there anything else? We are going to be late."

"What's happening?" she asked. "Where are we going?"

She looked around them, realizing that she was standing several floors up the Stalk, where they had landed on a wide, flat strip. A white tile covered the floor, and the glistening, polished metal of the Stalk was close enough to touch.

"We are on Floor 210 of the majestic Stalk," the android said. "Today we are hosting a group of wealthy travelers, all members of the families that originally funded the construction of the Stalk. They have requested to meet a few individuals from every part of the Stalk operation as well as from the town surrounding it."

"Yes, yes," Jack said. "I know that much." Everyone in town knew that they could be selected at any point and most considered it an honor—except for those that worked at the Hole. The knew it was a curse. 80% chance of death.

"What do you want to know, then?" the android asked. "Or can we go?"

"Who am I meeting? Where are we going? What am I supposed to do?" Jack spouted off a list of questions that she didn't really care so much about the answers to, just that gave her precious time needed to think of something, anything. She didn't want to go through the door.

The android looked at her with thinly veiled impatience. "You're meeting guests of the Stalk, now, in Room 210-10, and you are supposed to nod and smile and answer their questions politely."

"What if I don't want to?" she asked.

"Then you will be fined and jailed for violating the terms of your citizenship."

"Oh." That clearly wasn't an option. She needed something else, anything. "What if I don't want to meet them in Room 210-10? I'd rather go to the base of the Stalk, meet them on solid ground."

"That is non-negotiable," the android said. "What if... if..." Her mind scrambled for something—anything. "—if I don't want to walk through that door?"

The android stared at her for a moment and shook its head ever so slightly. "I suppose then, we could walk through a different door."

The android turned left and began to lead Jack along the outside of the building on a path between the wall of the Stalk and the hover landing area. Jack looked back toward where Leroy was climbing into the Bubble. He grinned and gave her a thumbs-up.

Jack shook her head. She wasn't planning on dying, not if she had anything to say about it.

Jack had always imagined the inside of the Stalk to look a bit gritty and dirty, with strands of living metal winding their way up through the middle, keeping the structure both solid and fluid at the same time. Maybe there were a few nicer rooms where the rich people visited, but most of it was just metal and dirt.

Her imagination couldn't have been more wrong. Everything was perfectly, glisteningly clean. There wasn't a speck of dirt or a smudge of grease anywhere.

The ceiling, walls, floors were shining silver, and paintings depicting stars, planets, houses, and animals hung on the walls—there was such wide variety of illustrations that Jack couldn't even begin to guess what the connection was between them all.

The android led her through gleaming halls with high vaulted ceilings to a room with a large table in the center with four people staring at her.

"This is Jack," he said. "Please wait here while I let our guests know you've all arrived."

Jack took the one empty seat. The woman next to her had her mouth open, and the others looked at her a bit nervously, as if she had startled them somehow. The only one who didn't look shocked was a woman sitting across the table from her chewing her nails and glaring stonily into the distance.

"What?" Jack asked, annoyed at the stares.

"You're from the Hole." The woman that spoke had her hair in a tight bun and a disapproving look on her face.

"Yeah, so?" Jack scowled at her. "I'm not going to die."

"That's what they all say," said a man across the table from her, wearing a plaid shirt and baseball cap. He was chewing a toothpick.

"What do you mean, 'they all'?" Jack asked. Had he met the others?

"This is my fourth time up the Stalk," he replied. "All of you Diggers have said the same thing. Only one that was different was Murphy."

"What'd he do different?" she asked.

"Not much." The man shrugged. "Just kept touching the walls."

Jack scowled. That was not helpful. "Who are you people anyway?"

"Tallis," he said. "Give hover tours of the Stalk."

"You know Leroy?" Jack asked.

"Best hover driver I've ever met," Tallis said with a grin. "He's a regular ace. Real friendly, too."

Jack decided that maybe she liked Tallis after all. "Yeah."

"Lucretia," said the woman with the tight bun. Her clothes looked extremely expensive, and though her jewelry was simple, it screamed wealth. "I manage the gift shop and give tours of floors 1 through 12, and I can't believe they let riffraff like you up here. These are the owners of the Stalk, the funders, the richest of the rich! What could they possibly have to say to Diggers?"

"Riffraff?" Jack snorted. "You sound like you're five centuries old with a stick up your butt. What could they possibly have to say to you?"

"You look like a wastrel, a thieving, conniving mud-sifter." Lucretia gave an exasperated huff and looked away.

Jack glanced down. She was wearing what she wore everyday—cargo pants (because she could never get enough pockets), her work boots, and a fitted tank top with a button-up shirt over it. "I look like I actually work for a living," she retorted.

"Anyway, I'm Mason," the next person said, interrupting the insult slinging. He looked nice, Jack thought—messy brown hair, simple khaki pants, and a t-shirt. He had his feet kicked up on the table, hands behind his head. "I do maintenance."

"On the Stalk?"

"Nope. On the Androids, third and eighth generations."

"Really?" Jack frowned. "How many Androids are there in here?"

" 'bout four thousand," Mason said, "give or take."

"And they have a lot of problems?"

"Older models are constantly breaking," Mason replied with an easy grin. "Some idiot decided to use hydrogen batteries, and when the casing for the battery breaks down the hydrogen leaks out and gets into all the Android's internal parts—"

"Mason," Lucretia interrupted. "Nobody cares."

Mason nodded, grinning with self-effacing amusement, and turned his attention to the last person at the table. She was chewing her nails and surveying them all with an irritated look.

She said, "We're not supposed to be friends."

"We're just introducing ourselves," Lucretia replied snootily. "It certainly doesn't make us friends."

"Besides, we have to have some way to figure out who to leave behind in an emergency," Mason said, grinning and glancing pointedly at Lucretia. Jack smirked at the joke, but Lucretia just ignored it.

The girl glared at Mason and then looked around the room with narrowed eyes. "Fine. Ace."

"Nice to meet you, Ace," Tallis said. "What do you do?"

"Climber."

Mason's eyes widened. "A Climber! I could never do that!"

"Seriously!" Tallis said, leaning back and crossing his arms. "Kudos."

"What, pray tell, is a Climber?" Lucretia asked, looking down her nose at Ace.

Everyone looked toward Ace, but she just scowled.

"Someone who does exterior maintenance on the Stalk," Mason explained. "Climbs the outside to do it."

"How horrific." Lucretia shuddered. "And I thought Diggers were bad."

The door burst open and the android entered. "The guests are ready. You will be meeting them individually. Please, follow me."

Everyone stood up.

"Wait," Jack said. Everyone froze. She could hear Leroy in her head: *Don't let them push you around.*

The android sighed and turned to look at her. "Yes?"

"I thought we were VIPs."

"You are."

"So how come we didn't get food or water or anything? You just plopped us in an empty room and expect us to feel honored?"

The android looked at her for a moment, his stare burning a hole in her head. "We will have something prepared for you when you return from your interviews."

Jack gave a little smile, and then stood up.

"I'll have to remember that little trick," Tallis murmured as he walked past her. "Maybe you won't die after all."

Just as she was about to step through the door, Jack reached out and touched an exposed piece of living metal. It felt warm. She pulled her hand away and touched it again. Still warm. What a strange thing, for metal to be warm, she thought. Shrugging, she put it out of her mind and stepped out into the hallway.

The android led them down a long hall. Every so often, Jack reached out her hand to touch the smooth, warm living metal that filled the inside of the building. She decided after a while that it wasn't exactly warm, but vibrating, which she still found rather unsettling. The walls in this hallway were empty—though still sparkling clean, there wasn't a painting or a scratch anywhere to be seen.

The android finally paused at a door. "Tallis," it said. "You will be meeting guests in this room."

"Sure thing," he said.

"Lucretia," the android said, ignoring Lucretia's question. "You are next."

"Wait a second." Jack frowned at the android, who sighed and turned to look at her.

"What now?"

"We want to stay together," she said.

"Yeah!" Tallis agreed. "We want to stick together." The others, except for Lucretia, murmured their agreement. Lucretia just sighed and crossed her arms.

"I'm sorry, that's not possible," the android said. "We don't have space for all of you to fit in the same room."

"We could go back to the room we just came from," Jack suggested, rolling her eyes at the obvious lie. There were only five of them, and it was a huge building.

"That is not an option," the android said.

"Aw, come on," Mason said, winking at Jack. "Work with us here!"

The android shook his head. "I suppose we could arrange for two of you go together."

"That would be better," Jack said. "What does everyone else think?"

"Much less stressful than going alone," Mason agreed. Everyone nodded and smiled.

"Fine." The android looked down at his clipboard and made some notes in the margin. "But there are five of you, which is an odd number."

"I'll go alone," Lucretia announced, looking down her nose at the others.

"You'll be here, then," said the android. "And I guess that means Tallis and Mason, you'll be together in the next room."

That left Jack and Ace.

"If you two will come this way." The android led them toward the next door in the hallway.

Jack glanced at Ace. She looked irritated, although Jack was pretty sure her expression hadn't changed much since they first met.

"Wait," Jack said.

Ace looked at Jack from the corner of her eye.

"What is it now?" The android spun around to look at Jack. "You might be VIPs but you can't just have everything you want."

Jack shrugged. "I don't want to go in that door yet. I want to go over there first."

She pointed to a door in the opposite direction the android was trying to take them. It was a plain door, with a sign on it that said, "Authorized Access Only."

"You're not authorized," the android said.

"Aren't you?" Jack asked.

"No," the android replied.

"I am," Ace said.

Jack looked at the Climber, mouth open. "You are?"

Ace shrugged. "I'm authorized everywhere. Let's go. Anything's better than these stupid meetings we have to go to." She strode rapidly toward the door, held out some kind of card under the keypad until it beeped, and then yanked it open, the android protesting in their wake.

The door slammed shut behind Jack, android stuck on the other side.

"What is this place?" Jack breathed.

The room was filled with monitors. Every monitor displayed security camera footage of a different place. She could see empty rooms and rooms filled with people, dark rooms and lit rooms, and when she stepped a little closer, she could see places around town too—the bakery, the grocery, the wristband repair shop.

"Can we have the room?" Ace asked the three guards who sat staring up at the screens. "Take a break."

"Sure thing, Ace," the tallest one said, grinning at her. He strode out of the room, followed by his two companions.

"What is this place?" Jack asked.

"Well," Ace said, "you've heard of the Watchers, right?"

"As in, the WIA?" Jack asked. "The Watchers and Inspectors?"

"That's them," Ace replied.

"Wait." Jack frowned. "I thought it was just a title because they paid attention to the goings on around the city and country and stuff. You mean they actually watch *everything* that goes on?"

"Yup."

Jack squinted at the screens, eyes flicking from one to the next. Then she froze. There it was: the Hole. On one screen, Jack could see Faith standing on the foreman's platform, like she always did, and on a different screen, she could see Petrov and Shelly tossing bags of dirt into the gaping chasm. The next screen was black, but with flickers of light flashing in and out at random points.

"What's this?" she asked.

"Inside the Hole," Ace replied.

"Why are they so interested in the Hole?" Jack asked. "There's just one screen for the bakery," she pointed up, "one for the gift shop, one for the coffee bar—but three for the Hole."

Ace glanced over at Jack. "The Hole is part of the Stalk."

"Really?" Jack frowned.

"It's a big secret though," Ace replied. "So don't mention that I told you."

"Any other big secrets I should know about?"

"Hmmm." Ace pursed her lips. "Well, Lucretia is pregnant."

Jack shook her head. Of course she was.

"This town is the only populated city on the planet."

"Wait, what?"

"Mason is recently single."

"Wait, go back," Jack said waving her hands around. "What do you mean? What about Boulder and Tall Lake and Journey City?" Wasn't Leroy's sister living in Journey City?

"All fake," Ace replied. "The people who 'visit' go to holo-simulators. It's a big secret."

"But, when the planet was settled, they sent twelve colony ships and set up twelve cities all over," Jack pressed. "What happened to them?"

"They're all dead," Ace replied. "But no one knows what happened to them, not even the WIA, or else they're keeping a pretty tight lid on it."

Jack had moved to the planet six years ago, with a dream of living a better life than her parents had. They had run a small fast food shop and worked in a hot and sweaty room for their entire lives, selling food to angry customers, and paying outrageously high taxes. Then her father had died and the state had taken the business away to pay the death tax. Jack's had mother moved into a homeless shelter and refused to leave, and her sister had boarded a different colony ship than Jack, and they hadn't seen each other since.

During the journey, she had met other people coming to this planet to find their parents and kids and relatives. What had happened to them? Had they all died too? Or were they just living here, in this one town? Or did they never arrive to begin with?

Her mind reeled.

"What do you mean no one knows what happened to them?"

"One day," Ace explained, "a Hole opened up in the center of town. Then the people disappeared. That's all anyone knows."

"We have a Hole," Jack said. "We're still here."

"We feed the Hole." Ace raised her eyebrows. "Maybe it just hasn't gotten hungry enough yet."

The android banged on the door. "We have to go now!" it yelled.

"Where are the others?" Jack asked. She suddenly had an urge to make sure her new friends were still alive, and not being fed to the Hole in some sort of secret, dystopian ritual.

"There's Lucretia." Ace pointed at a screen all the way to the left.

Jack walked up to it and pressed the volume button.

"I've put in dozens of complaints," Lucretia was saying, her sparkling earrings dangling back and forth. "We have got to look into increasing the cost of visiting the Stalk. I mean, with guests of a pedigree like yours, we can't just have any ruffian mongrel wandering around, now can we?"

Jack turned the volume off immediately. "Wow, she's annoying."

Tallis and Mason were on the next screen.

"We lost one last week," Mason was saying. "He jumped off the outside, said he was aiming for the Hole. It didn't make any sense to the rest of us—we tried to stop him but…"

"Too bad, really," Tallis said. "There were some Flyers out, but none of them were fast enough to catch him."

"But sometimes the software errors just go right down to the base code, and you can't do anything to stop them," Mason explained. "And that one worked higher than anybody else. I can't say I understand, but I might jump too if I started workin' up there."

The banging on the door intensified. "We have to go!" the android called again.

"We can get in here whenever, right?" Jack asked.

"Just say the word." Ace grinned. "If you're trying to break rules, I'm game. Just gotta tell me what you're trying to do."

Jack headed back to the door, pausing to reach out and touch a bit of exposed living metal. It hummed under her touch, and she suddenly felt like it wanted to touch her, like it needed her to touch it. She pulled her hand away quickly and shivered.

"Yeah that's why I work with gloves on," Ace said, and led Jack out into the hallway.

The android led them to an empty room with two large couches and a table between them.

"Which couch do you think doesn't have a camera pointed at it?" Jack asked.

Ace shrugged. "They can probably just move the camera."

It was a good point. Jack began to pace around the outside of the room, periodically reaching out to touch the walls or the back of the couch. She wasn't going to sit down at all, she decided. That was obviously what they wanted her to do.

"Please have a seat," the android said.

"I don't think I will," Jack replied, taking slow, long strides.

Ace plopped down on one of the couches and put her feet up on the coffee table.

The android stared at them for a moment, and then left the room, closing the door with a bang.

A few minutes later, the door opened, and tall, graceful woman wearing a long purple, shimmering gown glided into the room and looked back and forth from Ace to Jack.

"I thought I was just meeting with Ace," she said.

"We didn't want to split up," Jack said.

"I see that." The woman looked thoughtfully at Jack for a moment, and then moved forward and sat on a couch. "Well, my name is Jasmine, of the Solv Family. I'm here inspecting the Stalk. I'd like to ask you a few questions."

"We'd like to ask you some questions too," Jack said.

Jasmine looked mildly surprised, but nodded. "Of course. I'd be happy to answer any questions you might have."

Jack wandered past the couch where Ace sat and touched the opposite wall. It tingled this time, a little less like a vibration, and a little more like, well, electricity. Like touching an electric fence.

"Why are you here?" Jack asked.

"I came to talk to Ace," Jasmine replied. She turned to the Climber. "How are you doing, Ace? It's been a while since we've heard from you."

"Fine," Ace replied, crossing her eyes.

Jack looked back and forth between them curiously. They knew each other?

"Any idea when you'll be coming home?" Jasmine asked.

Ace shrugged. "I've got a lot of work to do."

"Someone else can do that work," Jasmine replied, looking slightly—elegantly—annoyed.

"Not as well as me," Ace said.

Jack watched them with fascination. Jasmine's make-up was perfect, not a line or a hair out of place. She had done the modern thing where she put little dots under her eyes and down her nose, and wore a dark purple lipstick contrasted sharply to her pale features. Her hair was also dyed purple, to match the lipstick, Jack presumed, and the hat a peach-colored flat thing tacked tightly to the hair. Ace on the other hand, seemed to have gone drastically in the opposite direction. Her shirt and pants were all black, too big, and filthy, like she hardly ever washed her clothes. She chewed her fingernails, which were also painted black, and wore no make-up at all.

"Look," Jasmine said, fluttering her eyes. "Your father is about to disown you. He was willing to forgive some youthful rebellion, but it's been nearly three years!"

"Let him disown me!" Ace exclaimed. "What do I care?"

"You should care!" Jasmine put her hand up to her neck and swallowed, like she was doing everything within her power to stay calm. "He had a heart attack last year! And you didn't even come!"

"I sent a card." Ace shrugged. "Flying is expensive."

"We would have paid!"

"Is this really what you came here to talk to me about?" Ace asked. "To berate me because I didn't come home?"

"He could have died!"

"I could die every day," Ace replied. "And no one shows up to say hi, except for you, once a year, during this stupid pilgrimage to make sure the Stalk is still growing!"

"You made the choice to be here," Jasmine chastised.

"And you make the choice to keep dumping money into this… this… alien thing, and for what?"

"You know why," Jasmine said, glancing at Jack.

"Yeah, so you can get richer and richer!" Ace exclaimed, "while everyone on this planet dies!"

Jasmine stood up abruptly. "Well. I guess that's it then." She took a deep breath like she was trying to calm herself. "You've disowned us. I'll let your father know."

She turned and strode out of the room, the door slamming behind her.

"Ugh, what a horrible woman!" Ace exclaimed, a scowl on her face. "She things she can do whatever she wants, just because she owns half the galaxy!"

"Was that your mom?" Jack asked.

"Yup," Ace replied, scowling. "Self-righteous, rich, entitled, and best of all, stupid. Threatens to disown me every year but hasn't gotten around to it yet."

"What was all that about the planet dying?" Jack stepped forward and plopped down on the couch next to Ace.

Ace stared at her critically for a second. "Let's go for a walk."

She stood up and headed toward the door. Opening it, she peered out both ways before gesturing for Jack to follow. Jack stepped out into the hallway.

"Wait," Ace said. She reached out and ripped the ID bracelet off of Jack's wrist. The three beans still glowed. "Get rid of this." She tossed it back into the room they had just come from; Jack noticed that she didn't have one either.

"Um…" Jack looked back and forth between where her bracelet lay on the floor and Ace. "You know how much those things cost to get replaced?"

"If you really decide you want it," Ace said, "I'll get you a new one. Now let's go."

Jack followed her through the halls, gleaming silver. This part of the Stalk was nice, clean, and had rugs on the floor. Then they reached a door that read, "NO ENTRY," in big bold letters. Ace ignored the sign and swiped her card, pushing through.

The other side of the door was just another hallway, but it was dark over here, hardly any lights. The walls were still glistening clean, but there was nothing else—no furniture, no rugs, no wall hangings, no nothing.

"Cleaning staff sure does a lot," Jack said, looking around. Even the ceiling was sparkling clean.

Ace let out a snort. "Cleaning staff? Ha! What cleaning staff?"

Jack frowned. "If there's no cleaning staff, how is this place so impossibly clean?"

"It cleans itself, obviously." Ace shook her head.

"I thought you cleaned the outside," Jack said, frowning. "And like, a bunch of other people."

"Well, yeah, that's because of the hydrogen outside. I mean, there's not that much, but the Stalk is very sensitive to it. It gets filtered out for the inside, but the Stalk can't do anything about it on the outside."

"They filter it out?" Jack raised her eyebrows. "There's hardly any hydrogen in the air—it can't possibly make that much difference."

"Well it does."

"What do they do with it then? The hydrogen?"

"Use it to make fuel cells for the androids, obviously." Ace pulled open another door and dragged Jack through. "Anyway, have you been to the actual elevators?"

"No," Jack said.

"Well," Ace said. "This is a space elevator, right? They keep telling everyone that the actual 'elevator' part is still in production, that they built this huge building out of living metal so it can flex with the turn of the planet, and there will be four cables running up the outside of all four corners eventually, to make it easier to launch ships or some nonsense like that."

"Yeah," Jack replied. Everyone knew that.

"Well," Ace said. "That won't ever happen because this isn't actually a space elevator."

A door in front of her slid open and revealed a small room.

"That looks like an elevator to me," Jack said, as Ace pulled her inside. She felt confused, like she was supposed to be grasping something she wasn't. A grand conspiracy? A weird alien secret?

"It's an actual elevator," Ace replied, tapping some buttons on the control panel. "But it's not a space elevator."

"What's it for then?" Jack asked.

"To get to the top."

The next moment, it felt like the floor had dropped out from underneath her. Jack shrieked and grabbed the wall, her stomach somewhere in her feet.

Ace whooped and grinned as the elevator soared upwards, faster than Jack could have ever imagined. She closed her eyes and gritted her teeth, trying not to be sick and begging the universe that it would be over soon.

And then it was.

The elevator stopped.

Jack stumbled forward, away from the wall of the elevator, and sank to her knees.

"Oh, come on," Ace said, grabbing Jack by the arm and pulling her to her feet. "It wasn't that bad."

"It was that bad," Jack replied, trying to take deep breaths to calm her racing heart. "It really was."

"Well, you're gonna love the trip down then."

"You do that all the time?" Jack asked.

"Nope!" Ace grinned. "That was my first time! Should've done it a long time ago, but I knew I'd get disowned as soon as I did. But I'm now that I'm officially disowned, I guess it doesn't matter anymore."

The elevator door slid open with a CLUNK and fresh air rushed into the small room. Ace stepped out into a large, wide open space. Dozens of people with large machines were working under a glass dome, above which, Jack could only see the sun, the moon, and the blackness of space. When she looked down, the spherical edge of the planet was visible but the town at the base of the Stalk was too small to be seen. She gasped and stepped back away from the edge. It was so far down and she was so high up, and the whole world seemed like it was getting farther and farther away and she was floating, just floating in the never-ending emptiness—

"Hey!" Ace grabbed Jack's arm and shook her. "Snap out of it! You're fine."

Jack blinked a few times and looked around her. The sun was actually quite bright, despite the blackness everywhere else, and as long as she didn't look over the edge, it was just another room on another level of the Stalk. Right?

She tried to focus her attention on the things going on around her.

"What is all this?" She frowned.

The top of the Stalk was marked out in squares, and each square had a person in it with some kind of machine. They would pull the machine through the square, and a thin layer of silver would peel up. Then, the person would lift the silver into a hover cart and transport it to a docking station on the far side of the dome, where a large spaceship was docked—probably, when she thought about it, the ship Jasmine had come on.

"Who are these people?" Jack asked.

"Androids, not people," Ace corrected.

The nearest android stopped what it was doing and walked over to where Jack and Ace stood.

"Display permissions, please," it intoned.

Ace held out her card.

"Permissions denied," the android said. "This is an off-limits area. You are not allowed."

"Am too," Ace said. "How else would I have been able to get on the elevator?"

"Permissions revoked..." the android paused, "exactly three minutes ago. Please return to the elevator."

"Revoked by who?" Ace demanded.

"By Jasmine Solv of the Kov Star System."

"Mom?" Ace exclaimed. "She revoked my permissions?"

"It was a pretty bad fight," Jack said, shrugging. "At least from where I was standing. We should probably go now."

Ace scowled and looked around the room. "We could take them."

"No, we couldn't," Jack replied, a knot growing in her stomach. "Let's just go." She grabbed Ace's arm and began to drag her back toward the elevator.

"This isn't the last you'll hear of me!" Ace growled toward the android.

"Noted," the android replied.

Jack dragged Ace back into the elevator and took a deep breath as the doors closed behind them. "What were they doing out there?" she asked.

"Harvesting," Ace replied.

"Harvesting what?"

Ace gave Jack a look. "Living metal, obviously. Where do you think it comes from?"

"I don't know," Jack said, shrugging. "Whatever planet they found it?"

"That planet imploded a long time ago," Ace replied. She reached out and hit a button on the control panel.

"Imploded?" Jack asked, and then the floor dropped out from under her feet and she was falling, and then there was nothing.

👽

When Jack woke up, she was in a dark room. Her head hurt, but otherwise, she seemed fine. She quickly counted her fingers and toes, then sat up.

"Ace?" she asked quietly.

"Shhhh!" Ace replied from somewhere in the darkness. Jack heard a scrabbling sound, and then she felt Ace grab her arm.

"Where are we?" Jack whispered. "What happened?"

"Well," Ace said, barely loud enough for Jack to hear, "you fainted. So thanks for that. I dragged you in here. And now the androids are after us."

"What?" Jack asked. "Why?"

"I didn't exactly go back to where we were supposed to be. We're on a mid-tier floor."

"What?!" Jack raised her voice slightly, and Ace reached out and clapped her hand over Jack's mouth.

"Be quiet!" she hissed. "They'll hear us!"

"Why are we here?" Jack demanded. "Why didn't you take us back?"

"I just…" Ace sighed. "There's something I can't figure out. And now that I have my permissions revoked, I won't have any more opportunities to dig around."

"Figure what out?"

"Okay, so you know how they're harvesting living metal from the top of the Stalk?"

"Yes." Jack's head hurt. She didn't think she was going to be able to figure this out any more than Ace, and all she really wanted to do was go home and go to bed and start the day all over again. But next time, she would avoid Ace at all costs.

"Well, Mom always told me that the Hole was how they were feeding the Stalk. All of the dirt and trash you Diggers dump into the Hole is consumed by the living metal and used to produce more living metal."

"Okay? So?" Jack shook her head.

"So they were filling the Holes at the other cities," Ace continued. "But now they're all dead. Why are they all dead? What happened to their Stalks?"

Jack shook her head. It was still hard to think about all the other cities on the planet that were just… gone. "I didn't think they had Stalks, did they?" she asked, trying to focus on what little she had learned about it in school. "At least, in history class we learned about just one Stalk. Just ours."

Ace frowned.

"Why do you care, anyway?" Jack asked. "Why are you even here?"

"It's a long story," Ace said, "but basically—"

She was interrupted as the lights flooded on. They were in a meeting room of some sort, with a rug on the floor, several chairs, a large table, and painting on the opposite wall. A holo figure appeared in the middle of the room—a woman, wearing fitted black pants and shirt, frowning. Ace grabbed Jack and ducked behind a couch.

"Holos can't see us!" Jack exclaimed.

"Yes, actually they can," Ace hissed. "And hear too."

"We are missing two guests, Ace the Climber and Jack the Digger," the holo said, voice booming in the silence of the room. If you have seen or heard from either of them, please inform the nearest android."

Then it disappeared.

"What do you mean they can see us?" Jack demanded.

"Just another strategy the Watchers use," Ace replied, shrugging. "I'm surprised that's not common knowledge yet—I tell everyone I meet."

"We have to go," Jack said, shaking her head. "They're going to…"

"Wait a second…" Ace interrupted, staring past Jack. She slowly rose to her feet, as if in a trance, and stepped toward a large painting hung on the opposite wall.

"They're going to find us!" Jack protested. "What if they put us in prison? Or kill us!"

"Jack," Ace whispered. "This is it!"

"What?" Jack asked.

"This!" Ace gestured toward the wall hanging. It was a painting weird-looking grey tree, with roots growing down into a large sphere. Jack stared at it a little more closely. The trunk, if it really was a tree, grew from the roots in almost a perfectly straight line, with only a few wisps of branches reaching out from it. The top was rounded and shone silver.

"It's a painting of a tree," Jack said.

"No," Ace said. "It's a painting of the Stalk."

Jack frowned. "What do you mean?"

"It's the Stalk!" Ace exclaimed, a little louder this time. She reached out a finger and pointed at the trunk of the tree in the painting. "That is the Stalk. The rounded part at the top is the dome."

"You're saying the Stalk has roots?" Jack raised her eyebrows. "That take up the whole planet?"

"Yes!" Ace exclaimed. "It has roots! That's what the Holes are!"

Jack frowned for a minute, processing this last bit of information. "It's a bit of a leap, don't you think?" she asked. Though it did explain why, even though they dumped dirt and trash into the Hole every day of the year it never seemed to get any fuller, and why they couldn't send cameras (or people) down into the Hole without them disappearing too. It also explained what happened to the other settlements—if the Hole got too hungry, maybe it ate the people that lived there too.

Slowly, Jack turned her attention from the painting to the wall beside it. It gleamed silver, sparkling and warm. She reached out a finger and touched it.

It buzzed, sparked, and then, almost like an echo in her brain, she heard the words: *I'm hungry.*

"It's hungry," Jack said, almost without realizing she was speaking.

"What is?" Ace asked.

"The Stalk."

Jack reached out and touched it again. *Hungry. Give me more.*

"It's hungry. Touch it yourself."

Ace frowned at her, then reached out and touched the wall herself. "I don't hear anything," she said, her frown deepening.

The door burst open. "There you are!" Jasmine exclaimed from the doorway. "You've got the androids all in a tizzy!"

"Mom!" Ace scowled at the tall, elegant woman, and crossed her arms. "You revoked my permissions!"

"I certainly did," Jasmine replied. "You've been here far too long. I'm taking you home with me."

"No!" Ace argued.

"I'm afraid you don't have a choice."

An android appeared from behind Jasmine and strode over to Ace. It grabbed her by the arm. "You're coming with us, now," it droned.

"No!" Ace exclaimed, reaching out to grab Jack's hand. There was something hard, square that she stuffed into Jack's palm.

"Yes," the android said, and then Ace just fell to the ground in a heap, unconscious.

Jack gasped, holding tightly to whatever it was Ace had given her.

"I'm so sorry you had to suffer through all of this," Jasmine replied, looking kindly toward Jack. "I will guide you back down to the others. We really appreciate all of the hard work you do for this community."

"Um, sure," Jack replied, watching with wide eyes as the android lifted Ace up over its shoulder and left the room.

"This way, please," Jasmine said.

Jack followed her down the hallway and back to the elevator, taking a brief moment to glance at her hand. Ace had given her her permissions card, though, though what good it would do now that Ace's permissions were revoked, Jack wasn't sure. Jack held her breath and closed her eyes as the elevator door slid shut behind them, but to her surprise, the trip was much shorter than she thought it would be. They exited the elevator into a long, sparkling silver hallway, and Jasmine led her to an empty room with several couches.

"Someone will be with you shortly," Jasmine said formally. "Have a wonderful day."

Jack sank onto one of the couches, filled simultaneously with dread and relief. Relief because Ace was gone and she wouldn't continue to be dragged into off-limit areas, and dread because she had no idea what was going to happen to Ace, and she now faced the problem of what the real story behind the Stalk was. When she had woken up earlier that day, she was filled with confidence, stubbornness, and a determination to not die like her predecessors had. But now, she felt like she was caught up in something much bigger and darker than she could have ever imagined.

Then a thought occurred to her. Two Diggers hadn't jumped—Murphy and Lisa. But they hadn't come back to the Hole either. The story circulating was that they had been promoted, taken off world somewhere. But what if they had died too, just some other way?

The door opened and Mason and Tallis strode in, plopping down in the chairs opposite Jack.

"Man, that was boring!" Mason exclaimed.

"Boring is right," Tallis said, kicking his feet up on the small table between the chairs. "Now I'm hungry."

"Yeah, where's that food the android promised us?" Mason asked, shaking his head.

"What happened in your meetings?" Jack asked.

"Not much." Mason shrugged. "We just met with five or six different people, and they all asked us the same questions—do you like working, how many hours do you do, what's the biggest problem you've had with the androids, what do you do with old batteries, how many batteries do you go through in a typical week—that sort of thing."

"Sounds boring," Jack said.

"What about you?" Tallis asked. "We saw the holo was looking for you."

Jack looked at him for a minute. She didn't know what to say. Should she just say it was the same? Or should she tell them about what really happened, about the top of the Stalk and about Ace getting carted away?

"Uh, we kind of went off book a little."

"Where's Ace?" Tallis asked. "She get lost?"

"It's a long story," Jack said. "Basically, her mom was here. She's from the Solv family."

"No kidding!" Mason exclaimed. "Won't Lucretia be pleased to hear that."

"Pleased to hear what?" Lucretia's voice came from the doorway.

Mason burst out laughing. "Tell her, Jack!"

"Tell me what?"

"Ace was a member of the Solv family," Jack replied.

"You can't be serious," Lucretia said, her face a look of disgust. "They are the wealthiest, most well-respected family in the galaxy. They would never allow one of their own children—"

"Well, they did," Jack replied. "And then disowned her, and then kidnapped her to take home with them."

"I should think so!" Lucretia exclaimed, settling into one of the chairs, as far from Jack as she could get. "You can't have that kind of youthful rebellion polluting your family name—certainly not!"

"What did you mean you went off book?" Mason asked, turning back toward Jack.

Jack looked at the others and then decided—why not tell them? If there really was some kind of issue with the Stalk eating entire towns, everyone should know. Everyone should have the option to leave if they wanted to—it was only right.

"Well, it turns out the Stalk is an alien," Jack began. She explained how Ace had taken her to the Watcher's room, and then about the fight with Jasmine. She told them about the ride up the elevator, and how Ace's permissions had been revoked, and the ride back down. She omitted the part about her fainting, and simply said they had ducked into a room to hide. Then she explained about the wall, how it was hungry, and Mason immediately jumped up and touched the nearest silver.

"I don't hear anything," he said.

"Ace couldn't either," Jack replied. She shrugged.

"Maybe that's why all the Diggers jumped," Lucretia suggested. "They got here, started hearing things, realized they were insane and worthless, so they jumped."

Everyone turned to look at Lucretia with varying expressions of disgust, anger, and disbelief.

"Wow," Tallis said. "What a shitty thing to say."

Jack stood up and strode over to where Mason stood, trying not to think about Lucretia. She might think Jack was worthless, but Lucretia was really the one who deserved to get dumped into the Hole. Jack shook her head, trying to clear that thought as well. No, Lucretia didn't deserve to get dumped into the Hole. No one did, no matter how terrible a person they were. Everyone deserved a chance at life, and Jack certainly wasn't qualified to make judgements about whether or not someone had used up that chance.

She reached out and touched the wall.

I need you. You are the most beautiful thing I have ever seen.

Well. That was different.

"What's it saying?" Mason asked.

"Um…" Jack shrugged. "It's not making sense."

"What's it say?" he pressed.

"I need you, you are the most beautiful thing I've ever seen," Jack repeated.

Everyone stared for a moment, confused.

"I thought it was hungry," Mason said.

"Me too," Jack replied.

"She's clearly making it all up," Lucretia huffed, shaking her head with scorn. "The Stalk is an inanimate object. It doesn't talk. She just wants attention."

"Can you talk back to it?"

Jack shrugged. She reached out to touch the wall again. It tingled under her fingertips. She thought very hard in the direction of the Stalk, *why are you hungry?*

It's been a year since I've eaten, the Stalk answered.

Jack jerked her hand away from the silvery metal and stared at it with wide eyes. "It worked!" she said. "I asked it why it was hungry and it told me it's been a year since it's eaten!"

"Don't you feed it every day?" Mason asked. "I mean, if the Hole is part of the root system."

Jack touched the wall again.

We feed you every day, she thought.

Dirt, the Stalk answered. *Mud. Trash. I want meat.*

"It wants meat!" Jack exclaimed, leaping back away from the wall.

Tallis gasped and Mason took a few steps away from the wall as well.

"Ludicrous," Lucretia said, shaking her head. "Utter nonsense. What small-minded people will do for attention never ceases to amaze me."

"Maybe we could just dump Lucretia in the Hole," Mason suggested. "Then it won't be hungry anymore."

"Well, I never!" Lucretia exclaimed. "It's no wonder you all work on the ground! Your lack of elegance and refinement clearly makes you unfit to deal with the high caliber of people I interact with every day!"

The room filled with chatter as Mason and Tallis began to argue with Lucretia, conversation devolving into insults and name-calling. Jack tuned out the noise and turned her attention back on the wall. She wanted to touch it. She wanted to know more. Slowly, she reached out and touched the wall again.

Immediately, the sounds of the room around her faded, and her entire attention was focused on the shining silver presence in front of her.

You're back, the Stalk said. *I've missed you, Jack.*

Jack swallowed. It knew her name. *How do you know my name?* she asked it.

I know you, it replied. Well, that was cryptic and less than helpful.

What kind of meat? Jack asked, switching tactics.

Yours. I've been smelling you for so long, and you smell delicious.

Jack shivered. Creepy. *I'm not just going to jump into the Hole,* she said.

You will, just like the others.

Not all the others. Murphy didn't. Lisa didn't.

They didn't want to, the Stalk said, *but, after all, that's what I have androids for.*

What do you mean?

They refused to jump, so I just enjoyed their company from right here.

Jack yanked her hand back from the wall. *From right here*, it had said. Did that mean... it didn't need the Hole to eat? It just needed to be touching its food source? She looked around at the sparkling clean walls and floors and remembered how few rooms had furniture or wall hangings—the rest were empty. Did the Stalk eat the dust that landed? The furniture that was sitting alone in rooms, unused? If she touched the wall again with her bare hands, would it start to absorb her? Consume her?

"Hey!" a voice cut into her panicked thoughts. "Jack, what's wrong?" It was Mason. He had grabbed Jack's arm and was shaking her.

"It's too clean," Jack whispered.

Mason looked around them. "Yeah, they've got a good cleaning crew."

"There's no cleaning crew," Jack whispered. "It cleans itself."

"Oh my god," Mason said with horror, as the realization of Jack's implication sank in.

It didn't matter if she jumped in the Hole or not. It could just eat her right here. Swallowing, she reached out a hand and touched the wall one more time.

Why me? she asked. Why not another human?

I've been tasting you, the Stalk answered, little pieces, every time you threw something down the Hole. I need you, Jack. I can't wait any longer.

Why don't you just eat me right now? she asked.

I want you to want me too, it said, softly, gently, as if it loved her. *Give yourself to me.*

And if I don't? What if I run away?

Then I will consume every living being left on this entire planet. The voice was suddenly angry, violent.

Jack yanked her hand away from the wall again and winced. It was almost physically painful to think about— if she tried to run away, it would eat everyone else. And if the painting of the stalk with its root system filling the entire planet meant anything, it could easily kill everyone here, and destroy the entire planet from the inside out.

What other option did she have? She had to jump— or stay here and be eaten like Mason and Lisa.

"What did it say this time?" Mason asked, eyes wide.

Jack shook her head. "Nothing," she said. "Nothing." She sank into an empty chair and tried to put a smile on her face. "Lucretia was right—I was just making it up."

"The gall!" Lucretia exclaimed, shaking her head.

Mason looked at her, frowning, about to ask a question, but then the android appeared in the doorway.

"Thank you all for coming. We appreciate your time. I will now lead you back to the hovercopters, which will return you to your homes."

Everyone stood and made their way toward the door.

"I know you heard it," a voice whispered behind her. She turned to see Tallis standing behind her. "We've all taken turns flying the Diggers here or back—me, Leroy, the rest—and you all say the same thing." He put his hand gently on her shoulder. "We will do anything for you—just tell me what you need."

Jack nodded and gave him a half smile. He knew. He knew that all the Diggers had jumped, because how could you say no? If you said no and stuck around, the Stalk would eat you here regardless. If you tried to run away, it would consume everyone else. That was probably how all the other colonies had died—a Digger had tried to run. And its root stalks ran all the way through the core of the planet. If only there was a way to save everyone, or to satisfy the Stalk's cravings so it would stop eating people. After all, it was a living thing too. Didn't all living things deserve a chance?

Jack stood up, almost mechanically, and followed the others through the halls of the Stalk. She had to figure something out, or else jump. Just as they were about to exit the building, she reached out and touched the warm silver one last time.

Please, it said, *come to me. I love you.*

Leroy landed the hovercopter in the same green lawn they had taken off from that morning. The sun was on the opposite side of the sky. Jack hadn't even felt or noticed the ride back from the Stalk. Her fear of flying seemed so small now, so far away. Instead, she was afraid of dying. She was afraid of making the wrong choice. She was afraid of everything.

"Jack," Leroy said in a soft voice.

Jack looked up and realized the copter had landed.

"We've been sitting here for ten minutes," he said.

"I'm so sorry," Jack said, shaking her head and reaching to unbuckle her restraints.

"Is there anything I can do?" Leroy asked, reaching out to touch her knee gently. "I've never had a Digger so quiet before. Usually they cried or talked—or at least made weird gasping noises. Even the ones that got promoted, Murphy and Lisa, they had a few things to say."

"They didn't get promoted," Jack said.

"What do you mean?"

She shrugged, a little helplessly. "They're dead too. Everybody's dead."

"What do you mean?"

"The Stalk ate them," she said. "But from the inside, not the Hole."

Leroy frowned, worry lines creasing the edges of his eyes. "It can do that?"

"Apparently." Jack shrugged. "I just don't know what else I can do, you know what I mean? It threatened to kill *everyone*—every living person on this planet! Unless I jump, of course." She shrugged again. "It doesn't matter if this town is the only one left on the planet, even losing this number of people to that miserable alien is too many."

"What do you mean we're the only town left?" A furrow creased Leroy's brow as his compassionate expression suddenly turned to a frown.

"Yeah, the Stalk ate the others."

"But what about the pictures and the news updates?" Leroy asked, his eyes widening.

"Holos."

His jaw dropped, and then his eyes filled with tears. "My… my sister…" He swallowed. "I thought it was strange I hadn't heard from her in quite a while, but I never expected… never… this…" Tears began to form in his eyes. "She's gone? Gone!"

"I'm sorry!" Jack leaned forward and wrapped her arms around the old pilot. She was crying too now. "I'm sorry."

After a few moments, Leroy's tears faded and he looked at Jack with an angry expression. "We have to kill it."

"I don't know how," Jack said, raising her eyebrows. She didn't want anyone to die, true, but was killing another living thing really the answer? She almost felt sorry for the Stalk, all alone like this on a planet of creatures that didn't understand it. "Besides, the Stalk's roots have penetrated the entire planet. If we kill it, the planet will probably implode, like its home planet did."

"Then we have to get everyone off," Leroy said. He brushed away his tears and set his jaw. "It's a two-step process: first, we get the people gone. Then, we kill it."

"But how?" Jack asked.

"Buckle in!" Leroy exclaimed. He turned back toward the controls and lifted off. "We've got work to do."

Jack grabbed ahold of the arms of her chair and held on tight as Leroy flew the copter at full speed, careening around buildings, flying barely high enough to even miss the tops of people's heads. Her stomach lodged somewhere in her throat. Then he soared up and over an entire row of businesses and came to a skidding halt in the courtyard of an apartment building several removed from Jack's. Another copter was parked, and Mason was just climbing out of it.

"Sam!" Leroy called out. "Mason! Over here! Quick!"

"Hey Jack!" Mason exclaimed, jogging over. "What's going on?"

"Get in!" Leroy ordered. "We need help!"

Mason climbed up and quickly strapped himself in, and the copter burst upwards.

"Mason, call Tallis," Leroy said, handing him the copter's com. "Tell him to meet me at the Perch. And tell him to bring Lucretia."

Jack was going to ask why Lucretia, but then the hovercopter soared over the tops of the nearby trees and the ground abruptly sank further and further beneath them. Instead, she closed her eyes, pictured Leroy's beard, and began to count the hairs. A few minutes later she though she felt Mason's hand rubbing her arm, and for a moment she could hear him and Leroy yelling back and forth at each other, but at the same time she remembered how high up they were and that the ground was so tiny and the people so tiny and the houses little pinpricks so she just counted hairs—

—and then Mason was shaking her shoulder. "Hey! We're on the ground!" He gently reached out and unbuckled Jack's restraints and then took her hand and guided her to the ground. "You okay?"

She nodded and took a few deep breaths. The ground beneath her feet felt very solid and comforting.

They stood in a grassy knoll a few miles outside of town. Several hovercopters were parked around a small cottage with a big sign over it that read, "The Perch."

"What's this place?" Jack asked, still feeling a little shaky from the ride.

"Secret hideaway for us copter pilots," Leroy replied. "We can all get here, but other folks can't. Our little secret."

He waved at Tallis who had just landed and was helping Lucretia unbuckle her restraints, and led them inside. It was dark, especially as the sun had set even further, and the inside was crowded. Several of the pilots laughed and greeted Leroy, and woman in a pair of leather boots carrying a big knife ran up and gave Leroy a kiss on the cheek before rushing out.

"Got a gutter snake!" she yelled over her shoulder.

"That's my wife, Liesl," Leroy said. "Her dad owns the place."

"Leroy!" A giant man with a beard so large it looked like an animal had taken up residence on his face thumped a massive mug of beer onto the counter with a bang. "Drink up!"

"Can we have the back?" Leroy asked, taking a swig as Tallis and Lucretia crowded into the bar right behind them, Lucretia with a scowl on her face.

"Sure thing," the man replied, jerking his head to one side. "I'll bring you a pitcher."

The back room looked like an event space, with a fancy rug and a big wooden table in the middle. Leroy chugged down the rest of his beer and then wiped the foam from his mouth, slamming the empty mug down on the table.

"Okay so you all know what's going on. We need to do two things: get everybody off this planet and kill the Stalk."

"Killing the Stalk should be second," Tallis said. "We should focus on the people first."

"How are we supposed to get the people gone," Mason asked, "if we don't have a colony ship handy?" He shook his head, brow furrowed.

"We could call one," Tallis suggested. "If we send out a signal, maybe a mercenary is close by."

"Signal is easy enough," Mason replied. "Anybody can call for a ride off planet whenever they want. It's just the deposit that's expensive. Anywhere we can get that kind of cash?"

"Borrow Lucretia's jewelry?" Jack suggested, half kidding and half serious. "Sell it?"

"Can I ask what I'm here for?" Lucretia cut in with a scowl. "You had no right to bring me here. I want to go home immediately."

"Wait a second!" Tallis exclaimed, his face lighting up. "We don't need to call for anybody!"

"What do you mean?" Leroy asked.

"There's a ship already here—the Solv ship that brought the funders! If we're really truly the only town, it should be big enough to hold everybody for a few weeks, and we can send out the signal from space—another ship should arrive easily within that time."

"You mean," Jack said, "we could potentially get everybody gone now? As in, today?"

"They leave in the morning," Tallis replied. "But yeah, if we can stop them, we have a way off planet."

"Ahem." Lucretia crossed her arms and raised her eyebrows. "I'm pregnant, you know. I can't be involved in all this running around."

Ace had been right, Jack noted. It was true, then— the Watchers were always watching. But how exactly could they get this specific? She looked down at her wrist where her band had been, flashing green beans only a few hours before.

"Wait." She put her finger to her lips. She pointed to her wrist and then grabbed Mason's hand. His band still had the three beans glowing. She ripped it off, ran to the nearest window, and threw it out. "They can hear us!" she exclaimed. "They know where we are and what we're doing."

"Who?" Leroy looked around frantically.

"The Watchers!" Jack could feel a sensation of panic rising in her chest. "They could be here any minute!"

Leroy stared at her for a second and then comprehension dawned. "They've always known…" he breathed.

"I guess we should plan fast, then." Tallis sighed and pulled his wristband off, tossing it out the window.

"These are expensive to replace!" Lucretia protested as Mason pulled hers off her wrist.

"Won't matter if the planet implodes," Jack replied.

A moment later all the bands had been fed to the wildlife living outside the bar.

"How do we get people onto the colony ship?" Tallis asked, looking around at the group. "We need to move fast in case they try to stop us."

"It's docked at the top of the Stalk," Jack said. "I saw it when Ace and I were up there. They're loading strips of living metal into it to take to other planets. If we can get people to the elevators on the outside of the Stalk, they can ride them up to the top and enter the ship that way."

"How do we tell people they need to go to the Stalk?" Mason asked.

"I've already got that figured out," Leroy said. He looked at Lucretia.

"What?" she asked.

"The holos," he replied. "You control those from the gift shop."

"Yeah?" she said.

"So, you can send out a message to everyone in the town, telling them to go to the Stalk, that it's dying, and the planet is going to implode. If they want to survive, they need to get to the Stalk as fast as possible."

"And," Tallis added, "there are dozens of copter pilots out there right now who can go to the furthest edges of the town and transport them to the Stalk."

"We should start now," Jack said.

"I'll take Lucretia to the gift shop," Tallis said.

"I haven't agreed to this!" Lucretia exclaimed. "I refuse to get involved!"

"You'll be safest at the Stalk," Jack replied. "You can be one of the first ones up. Please." She took Lucretia's hands in hers.

"I won't do it!" Lucretia crossed her arms and scowled at Jack.

"I'll do it," Tallis said. "I just need Lucretia's ID to get in."

"Take the bands we just threw out the window," Leroy said. "We'll keep her here."

Tallis rushed her out of the room, just as Leroy's father-in-law appeared with a pitcher of beer.

"Dad," Leroy said. "Can you keep her in one of the upstairs rooms?" He gestured to Lucretia.

"She's pregnant," Jack added, "so take care of her."

"Sure thing!" said Leroy's father-in-law.

"Someone'll have to take her to the Stalk shortly," Leroy added. "And I need to make an announcement to all the pilots out there."

"You can both come with me," said the enormous bearded man, leading them into the other room, Lucretia protesting the entire way.

Jack turned to look at Mason.

"I guess that means it's our job to figure out how to kill the Stalk," she said, her stomach turning over at the thought. She still wasn't sure she wanted to.

He smiled at her, and her stomach fluttered—too bad the chances of them surviving this were so low. She would have liked to have gotten to know him a little bit better.

"Poison?" he suggested. "Maybe dump some down the Hole."

Jack shook her head. "We dump all kinds of things into the Hole—old batteries, trash, compost, dirt—plus, if its root systems really do run through the entire planet, I'm sure it's at least gotten a taste of most of the poisons available on this planet."

Mason nodded, a thoughtful expression on his face. "Maybe we could—"

His thought was cut off by a crash and an explosion in the front. They ran out to the front where all the pilots were shouting and trying to get through the front door. A hovercopter had landed on the bar, crashing through the roof and one wall and landing on one side of the room. Leroy's dad was shouting as the person driving climbed out and staggered across the room.

"Ace?" Jack exclaimed.

"Jack!" she shouted. "They're coming! The Watchers are coming! They heard you plotting against the Stalk! Everybody get out!"

"Leroy!" Jack called. "Let's go!" She turned to Mason. "We'll have to wing it."

"I'm in."

They pushed through the crowd of pilots and sprinted toward Leroy's copter. Ace climbed in beside them, as the copter burst into the air. All around them, androids were landing on the ground and running into the Perch.

"They can fly?" Jack exclaimed.

"Yeah," Mason said, shrugging. "The new models, at least."

"Go, go!" Ace exclaimed. "Before they see me!"

She ducked down, hands over her head. Jack closed her eyes and tried not to think about flying.

"What's the plan?" she shouted to Leroy.

"I told the pilots," Leroy said. "They're on their way to the outer limits of the town and surrounding countryside to bring the people in. Did you figure out how to kill it?"

"No!" Jack shook her head, eyes still squeezed shut. "Just take us to the Stalk—we'll figure it out when we get there."

"How'd you get away from your mom?" Mason asked curiously, looking at Ace.

"I woke up on board the ship," Ace said, shaking her head. "I literally jumped out of the loading dock, hijacked an android, and used it to take the elevator down to the hovercopter landing pad. Then I stole one and flew it toward the coordinates my permissions card was giving off."

Jack touched her pocket where the card was. She had forgotten she had it.

"With an entire contingent of androids on your tail," Mason added.

"I'm lucky I got to you," Ace said.

They drove in silence for the next few minutes. Jack had no idea how close they were to the Stalk. Then Ace called out, "Take us to level 12! I programmed the lock on that door so I can get in or out without my permissions. And the gift shop is only two floors down. We can find Tallis."

"There's no landing strip there," Leroy replied. "You'll have to jump."

Jack opened one eye and saw that they were flying in a large arc around the Stalk. She felt her stomach drop, but there was no other way. She swallowed and focused on the image of Leroy's beard she was holding in her mind. Then the hovercopter slowed and held steady in the air.

"I'll go first," Ace said. "Jack, you have to watch so you know how to do it."

Jack swallowed and opened her eyes. The Stalk was only a few feet away. A small ledge with a railing jutted out with a door on one side leading into the Stalk. Ace unstrapped herself and moved to the edge of the copter. She sat down on the edge with her feet hanging over and launched herself forward onto the ledge.

"I can't do that," Jack whispered.

"Sure you can," Mason said, smiling at her.

"I'll get as close as I can, sweetheart," Leroy said. "Just position yourself, okay?"

Mason undid her straps and helped her slide out of her seat and onto the floor. "Don't look at the ground," Mason said. "Just look at Ace. She's going to catch you, okay?"

Jack nodded. Her stomach was in knots and her hands were shaking. She couldn't do it. She knew she was going to fall. But really, if she thought about it, was falling to the ground and dying any worse than being consumed by the Stalk, which would probably happen anyway? She took a deep breath. "Okay," she said.

Leroy moved the copter a little closer to Ace. It was only a few feet.

"I'll catch you!" Ace shouted. "Hurry!"

"Just push yourself forward," Mason whispered in her ear. "Everything is going to be alright." He gave her a little shove.

Jack screamed as her body flew through the air and landed with a thump on the ledge. Ace was there grabbing her arms and helping her stand. Jack's heart was racing, her mind spinning as if she couldn't breathe. The next moment, Mason was there beside her, his arm around her shoulders.

"Let's go!" he said, pulling her through the door and into the Stalk.

Ace dragged Jack into the Stalk. A feeling of relief washed over her as the walls of the building blocked out the view of the ground below. Jack knew it was irrational to feel safer inside of an alien that was trying to consume both her and an entire planet than simply being high above the ground, but it didn't matter. She would rather be in here any day.

"We're safest in the hallways," Ace said. "They don't install cameras in most of them, unless you're in the areas that have tour groups. The stairs are this way." She hurried off down the darkened hallway.

"We need to figure out how to kill the Stalk," Mason said intently, following close behind her. "Jack says they feed it everything. Is it even possible? Or should we just get all the people off the planet?"

"If I jump in that would sate it for a while," Jack said. She suddenly had a strange feeling. How had she gotten here? To this place? This time? Yesterday she had gotten up and gone to work like any other day. And this morning, she came to the Stalk vowing that she wouldn't die like the others. Now, she was *volunteering* to jump in the Hole. "Give us enough time to get everyone off world."

"That's a last resort," Ace said, shaking her head. She pulled open a door and began to take the stairs two at a time.

"Why don't you just ask it?" Mason said, looking back at Jack.

"Then it'll know I'm here."

"It probably already does." Ace shrugged, glancing up at them. "If it's really as intelligent as it seems, it probably already knows."

Jack paused mid-stairwell, took a deep breath, and reached out to touch the wall.

You're back.

She yanked her hand back. "I hate how it can do that," she whispered. Then she reached out to touch the wall again. *How do I kill you?* she asked it.

You can't, it replied. *I am eternal.*

"It says we can't kill it," she told the others. She felt a tiny sliver of relief. Maybe they shouldn't kill it—it was a living thing too. Maybe they should just get everyone off world and leave the Stalk alone.

"I don't believe it," Ace said. "If I have to clean rust off the outside every day to protect it from the negative effects of hydrogen, then at very least we know it's got a weakness, and anything with a weakness can be killed."

"Hydrogen?" Mason asked, frowning as if in thought.

"Yeah," Ace said. "It like burns it or something."

"Well, if hydrogen hurts it," he continued, "why don't we just drop a bunch down the Hole?"

"How?" Ace suddenly looked interested.

"The androids." Mason shrugged. "Their batteries are made from the hydrogen that's filtered out of the air."

A smile grew on Ace's face. "That's it!"

"How though?" Jack interjected. "How do we get them into the Hole?"

"We just have to piss them off," Ace said, excitement growing in her voice. "We just have to make them angry enough and they'll follow us. Like they did when I escaped!"

"How?" Jack asked again.

"Aren't they kind of already after us?" Mason suggested. "Because the Watchers heard us planning?"

"Let's make sure the message gets out first," Ace said. "Then we'll get to the top and lead them away. Tallis and Leroy can meet us up there with their hovercopters."

She turned and hurried down the stairs as quickly as she could, taking them three at a time now. Jack hurried to keep up. The whole situation seemed a little ridiculous, she thought. She laughed a little to herself. A space elevator made of living metal? That was evil and destroying the planet she lived on? Ridiculous. But somehow also very, very real.

They burst out into a beautifully decorated hallway. To their left was the Gift Shop. Tallis was there, fighting with Lucretia's wristband.

"I got it," Mason said. He took the band, fiddled with the settings, and the door clicked open.

"So glad you guys are here," Tallis breathed. "I thought I was never gonna get in."

"Jack!" Ace exclaimed. "You're the Digger. You send the message." She dragged Jack into the back of the shop where the holo-generator sat in the corner of the room. "Just stand in the center there."

Jack stepped up onto the platform as Ace turned it on. It began to hum and buzz.

"When I say now, you start talking."

"What do I say?" Jack asked.

"Just tell them what's going on. Focus on the important bits: the Stalk is destroying the planet, everyone needs to get here to escape on the colony ship."

Jack nodded. She was not prepared for this. It was like public speaking. She did not enjoy public speaking.

"Just pretend you're talking to me," Ace said. She smiled. "Now."

"What?"

"Now!" Ace exclaimed. "Go!"

"Oh." Jack looked into the light shining on her. "Um," she began eloquently. "My name is Jack. I'm a Digger." She looked at Ace, who was gesturing fanatically.

"Hurry up!" Ace mouthed.

"All the Diggers before me are dead," Jack said. "Jumped in the Hole. Because the Hole feeds the Stalk, and the Stalk threatened to kill all of you if we didn't jump. I'm not jumping. I'm gonna kill it, but I'm afraid it will try to kill you. So get to the Stalk quick. A ship is docked at the top—it will take you safely away from here. Just hurry."

Ace jumped onto the platform next to Jack. "I'm Ace from the Solv family. That's our ship up there. I'm issuing my invitation for you to board if you don't want to risk dying on this planet. Hovercopters are waiting at the outlying cities to fly you in. All I have to say is this: don't wait. If you want to live, come now."

She looked at Jack and shrugged. "That's all we can do. Let's go kill the Stalk." She grabbed Jack's hand, pausing only to hit send on her way past the controls.

As they stepped out into the main part of the gift shop, Jack looked to see a version of herself flickering. "My name is Jack," it said. "I'm a Digger."

"Let's go," Ace said. Mason and Tallis were waiting.

"But what's next?" Jack asked.

"We have to get to the top," Ace said. "That's where all the androids are, after all, right?"

"We can take the elevator," Mason said.

"How? My card doesn't work," Ace replied.

"Lucretia's will, right?"

They ran over to the closest elevator.

Tallis hang back. "I'm going to get my hovercopter. I'll meet you up there. And I'll tell Leroy what's happening." He ran off as Mason fiddled with Lucretia's band. The elevator beeped. They waited as it made its way up. When the door slid open, it was filled with people.

"Hurry!" one of the people said. "Did you see the message? I came as soon as I could."

"You're the Digger on the holo!" another one exclaimed. "I recognize you."

Jack nodded, feeling rather small, not worthy of recognition. "We need to get to the top too, she said."

"Make room! Make room!" Everyone squeezed around, shifting to make more room for Ace, Mason, and Jack.

Then the doors closed behind them, and the elevator began to rise. It was slower than last time, probably because of the weight of the extra people, Jack thought.

"How'd you get the elevator to work?" Ace asked.

"I'm here!" said a voice from the back. "Kat! Climber!"

"Oh good!" Ace said. "Can you get the other Climbers to help people evacuate?"

"Workin' on it!" Kat replied.

When the reached the top, Jack took a deep breath and tried to remember not to look over the edge at the curve of the planet below. Everyone crowded out of the elevator.

"Display permissions, please," one of the androids said, but there were too many people shouting and calling out; they rushed right past the android. Then a second elevator and another crowd of people swarmed out of it.

"We're here to get on the ship!" someone yelled, dragging a suitcase across toward where the ship was docked. "The Solv girl said we could!"

"Display permissions, display permissions," the android repeated desperately.

"If we display our permissions they'll start chasing us," Ace said, "and that will clear path for people to get to the ship."

"We have to wait until Leroy and Tallis get here," Jack replied. "Or else we'd just be jumping off the building. We have to get the androids to the Hole."

"The loading dock is over that way!" Ace yelled, pointing. The crowd began to surge across as the third elevator door opened and another crowd pressed their way out.

"One of us has to stay here," Mason said, "to help people get safely onto the ship."

"Can you reprogram a couple of the androids to help?" Ace suggested. "Just one? Or two?"

Jack looked around. The fourth elevator was just opening up and the top was officially crowded. There were probably a hundred or more people at the top of the Stalk, not counting the androids also taking up space.

Mason strode over to the android asking for permissions. "I'm Engineer 66115, please show me your code."

The android opened its hands and a holo-screen rose up, revealing lines of numbers and letters. Mason began to speak softly, to the android, giving a specific set of commands. Jack couldn't understand anything that the android was saying, but it clearly worked. The screen disappeared, and the android began to call out instructions for guiding the people toward the ship.

"Can you reprogram them to jump into the Hole?" Jack asked as he returned.

"Unfortunately, no," Mason said regretfully. "I only have control over a few basic functions—cleaning, repairs, and guidance. I can't make them do anything outside the Stalk."

"I could have," Ace said, shrugging. "But not with my clearance revoked."

Jack nodded. It looked like they were going to have to do what they said. "Let's head over there," she said. "We won't show our permissions until the last second. Mason, you stay here. Help people board and hijack a couple more androids if you need them."

"You got it," Mason replied.

"The Climbers are helping operate the elevators," Ace said. "That should be all you need."

"Make sure Leroy's family gets here safe," Jack added.

Ace and Jack slowly drifted toward the other side of the building. There was a very small landing strip outside, where Leroy and Tallis could land long enough for them to climb aboard.

"We should each go separately," Ace said. "If they have two ships to follow, there will likely be more of them."

Jack nodded. She tried to peer over the edge, but immediately became dizzy and pulled back, taking a few deep breaths.

"I'll watch," Ace said.

Jack nodded and turned to look back at the crowd of people filling the top of the Stalk. The first elevator had arrived again, and another group of people had begun to fill in the gaps. A few had started to go on board the ship. Jack began to do math in her head. If there were four thousand people living in their colony, and twenty-five could come up in each of the four elevators—so a hundred people at once—it would take a minimum of thirty trips up and down to get everyone—assuming each elevator was filled to the maximum, and everyone got here as quickly as they could… She shook her head to clear it. She couldn't think about that right now. She had a different task—kill the Stalk. Jack only hoped that the hydrogen from the androids' batteries would be enough. After all, they couldn't possibly know how many androids they would need.

"They're here!" Ace yelled. She reached out and took Jack's hand. "I'll help you get on first," she said, "and display our permissions. Where's the ID card I gave you?"

Jack handed it to her as the Bubble and Tallis' hovercopter both appeared above the ledge. Ace gave Jack a hand, and helped her climb in. Jack forced herself to stare at Leroy's stern, slightly red face and not the ground, far, far below them.

"We have to hurry," Leroy said. "Once we leave this protective dome then we won't have air for a short period of time—we're too high up."

"How'd you get up here?" Jack asked, shocked.

"I held my breath," he said, shrugging.

"They're coming!" Ace yelled, sprinting toward Tallis' hovercopter. "Go! Go!"

The androids had swarmed out of the door onto the ledge behind her and were staring as she leaped into Tallis's copter.

"Can't hang around, I guess," Leroy said.

"What if they don't follow us?" Jack asked.

"Then we'll come back."

Jack held tightly onto her seat as they blasted forward, Leroy gripping the controls tightly. She turned to look. Ace and Tallis had catapulted down and over, and the androids were still standing, staring.

"It's not working," she whispered, but then one of them leaped, flying through the air and following their trail. Then another jumped and another, until a legion of them were rushing toward them. Another stream followed after Tallis and Ace, like little spaceships in tuxedos.

"Call the Hole," Leroy said, handing her his com.

"What?"

"Tell them we're coming. Ask how far the dampener reaches."

There was a helpful button on the com labeled, "Hole." She pressed it. "This is Faith."

"Faith," Jack said. "It's Jack. How far does the dampener reach?"

"Jack?" Faith asked. "You better not be planning on jumping like the others."

"I'm not!" Jack exclaimed. "Just tell me!"

"Fifty feet." Faith sounded annoyed.

"Fifty feet," Leroy muttered. "We'll be cutting it close."

"Faith," Jack continued. "We're coming. Bringing the androids. You better run. Get to the Stalk before the planet explodes."

"What—" Faith began but Jack hung up.

"I don't like Faith," she said to Leroy.

And then her eyes locked on the ground. The curve of the planet was green and blue and white, and getting bigger and bigger. Then suddenly they were immersed in a cloud of white; water droplets covered the outside of the hovercopter all around them. Jack felt dizzy.

"Just a bit longer!" Leroy called. "Oxygen incoming!"

They emerged from the cloud and the ground was so close, yet still so far away. She could see the buildings, little squares, little shiny vehicles all on the ground, a crowd of them at the base of the Stalk. And the ground kept getting bigger and bigger as they rushed toward it—then Leroy switched directions and aimed them toward the Hole. She could see that too, a big gaping spot of blackness and darkness that filled and entire block, and she could hear it, too—*Jack,* it was saying. *I can feel you, Jack, so close. Come to me.*

She shook her head, trying to drown out the sound, and then they were close, so close—the Hole looked so big from up here. Jack looked behind them—sure enough, a crowd of androids was flying toward them, angry expressions on their faces, intent on getting to them. She could see Tallis driving nearby, his ship neck and neck with Leroy's, another swarm of androids in their wake.

"Unstrap." Leroy said as he began to weave between buildings.

"What?" Jack exclaimed.

"You might have to jump," he replied. "In case I bring it in too low."

"Jump?" If Jack's heart hadn't been pounding already, it was now. Blood rushed into her face and her chest constricted. "I can't—"

"It's that or die," Leroy said. "If I can't stop in time and the hovercopter flies within reach of the dampeners, you have to be ready to jump."

Jack nodded, swallowing. There wasn't really a lot of choice. She saw that he had already removed his straps and was sitting loosely in the pilot's seat.

"Now!" he exclaimed. The Hole loomed under them, dark, ugly, hungry.

She looked behind them. The androids were swiftly gaining on them, but quite a few were tailing a good distance behind. She unclasped her straps, hands shaking.

"Slow down," Jack said, heart pounding, hardly believing what she was saying. "The androids have to catch up."

Leroy glanced over his shoulder and nodded, decreasing their speed just enough that they began to catch up. Tallis copied them in his hovercopter.

"This is it," Leroy said. They were headed directly toward the Hole. "I'm going to yank up at 50 feet, sudden reversal. If it doesn't work, wait until we're just a few feet above the ground, and then jump, okay?"

Jack nodded, heart in her throat. She was going to die. She was pretty sure of it. At very least she could try not to though.

All at once, the Bubble jerked to a halt and began to slowly rise. The closest androids flew past them, lost control, and hurtled into the pit, but the others had slowed their descent.

"We... we..." Jack swallowed, her heart in her throat. "...have to keep going. Or they won't follow..."

Leroy nodded, face stern. "Alright," he replied. "Get ready to jump."

Jack held her breath as the Bubble began to lower again; then all at once, it was out of control, falling faster and faster, the gaping Hole getting bigger and bigger, blacker and blacker; somewhere in the distance she heard someone shout, "NOW!" and she closed her eyes, flung out her arms, and jumped. The wind rushed through her hair and she imagined the blackness getting closer and closer, bigger, hungrier, ready for her arrival. When she opened her eyes, she was hanging from the edge of the pit, Shelly holding onto one of her hands, and Petrov onto the other. She looked down. *I love you, Jack. You're so close.* The Hole was so loud here, thundering inside her skull. *I need you, Jack. Come to me. Just let go.*

"Come on!" Petrov shouted. "We have to go!"

Petrov and Shelly heaved her up and out of the pit and pulled her away from it. Androids fell like rain, crashing into the Hole and onto the ground all around them. She could see Leroy on the ground, where he had fallen when he jumped out of the Bubble.

"Wait!" Tallis exclaimed from nearby. He and Ace had crashed their hovercopter without it going down the Hole. "We have to feed it!" He grabbed the nearest android by an arm and dragged it toward the Hole. "We don't know how much hydrogen it will need to die!"

Petrov and Shelly looked at each other with mild panic but began to help anyway. Jack took a deep breath and headed for the nearest android. She dragged it toward the Hole and shoved it over the edge. This was something she was familiar with. This was what she had been doing for years. There would be no more jumping out of airplanes, or soaring through the air—instead, she could just focus on throwing things in the Hole.

They dragged android after android toward the Hole. It felt like an eternity as they just kept falling from the sky. Then she looked up. Dozens were hovering around the edge of the where the dampener could reach. Others had landed and were making a line around the edges of the fifty-foot radius.

"We'll never be able to get out of here!" Ace groaned, leaning down to help Jack grab another android and toss it over the edge. "Not with all of those 'droids making a wall between us and the Stalk."

"Can we increase the size of the dampener?" Leroy asked, heaving another one over the edge and into the Hole.

"Yeah!" Petrov exclaimed, face lighting up. He ran off toward the locker rooms.

Leroy paused as he walked past Jack. "I'd never be able to get used to being this close to the Hole," he said softly, shaking his head. "You're something else."

Androids suddenly began to rain again, falling into the Hole and crashing around them. Those that had been standing at the edge of the dampener fell down, unable to move. It had completely immobilized them.

"What is this dampener even for?" Jack asked, shoving one that had landed close to the edge in and watching it disappear into the blackness below.

"Keeping the androids away, probably," Tallis said. "So they couldn't poison the Stalk."

Then, the ground shook beneath their feet, a slow quake that jarred her to the core. Jack froze and looked at the others. They had also stopped what they were doing; Ace stared at the ground, a wide-eyed expression on her face which slowly turned into a smile.

"We did it," she whispered. "I think we did it!"

"We need to go!" Leroy exclaimed. "Now!"

Tallis tossed one more android into the pit, and then turned and began to run toward the gate, followed closely by Ace, Shelley, and Leroy. Petrov reappeared from the locker rooms and began to follow them.

Jack looked back over her shoulder at the Hole. It had been her life for so many years. Maybe she should stay, make sure enough androids had made it into really kill the thing. Something inside her wanted to stay.

"Come on!" Leroy said, stopping and gesturing for her to hurry up.

You need me too, the Stalk said. *Come back and I'll forgive you.* It was weak. She could hear it in its voice. And part of her wanted to go back. She knew what it was like to be on her own—it was just lonely, that was all.

"Don't listen to it." Leroy was suddenly by her side, holding tightly onto her hand. "Whatever it's saying, it's lying. Come with us."

"I could stay," Jack said. "Make sure enough androids end up at the bottom—" And maybe, if they needed more time, she could jump…

"No!" Leroy exclaimed. He dragged her toward the gate. "You're coming with us."

Don't go, the Stalk sounded so sad. *Don't leave me alone. I'm so alone.* Jack felt tears well up in her eyes.

I'm sorry, she called out in her mind. *Please forgive me.*

The Stalk didn't answer.

👽

It only took them a few minutes to sprint from the Hole to the Stalk, but the entire trip the ground rumbled and quaked under foot. Shelley tripped once but got up quickly; Petrov sprained his wrist when he fell but ignored the pain and stumbled on. At the bottom of the Stalk a crowd of people screamed and yelled, all trying to get off the planet at the same time.

Fortunately, there were only a few hundred left, and Jack saw that the hovercopters had arrived and were taking small groups of people to the top of the Stalk to take some of the pressure off of the elevators.

They were one of the last groups to climb on the elevator, which quivered and quaked as they rode it to the top. Jack shivered, imagining the Hole below—if the Stalk toppled over, would it fall in the Hole? Eat itself? It was a strange thing to think about.

When they reached the top of the Stalk, she saw Mason's eyes light up as he made his way over to them.

"You're back!" he exclaimed, wrapping his arms around Jack in a quick, tight hug.

Jack gestured to where she saw Jasmine being held tight by an android. Beside her was another woman, dressed similarly, and two men in bright red suits covered in living metal, all being held by androids.

"What happened to them?" she asked.

"They protested everyone trying to board." Mason shrugged. "Turns out they knew the Stalk was killing people, which is enough to cause the androids to take them into custody. Breaking the law and all that. Ace is next in line and will be taking command of the ship."

He turned to help guide Shelley and Petrov on board, along with the others rushing across the top of the Stalk. Jack held back, watching as the elevators emptied and more people ran in from the hovercopters. Leroy's wife and father-in-law appeared and he hurried over to them, tears in his eyes.

Jack reached out, feeling quite alone in the noise, and touched the soft, warm metal of the Stalk.

You betrayed me, it said.

You betrayed us, Jack replied.

I loved you, the Stalk said.

I'm sorry you have to die, Jack replied.

"Come on," Mason appeared in front of Jack and held out his hand. "Let's go."

She was the last to board the ship. The inside was dark and cold and crowded. Mason led her through the mob of people, all crying, talking, afraid, and up several levels until they reached a room with a large window that looked down at the planet below. In the ship, she realized, she didn't feel afraid, even though she was looking down at the curve of the planet so far below them, floating in the emptiness of space.

There was a loud crunching noise, and the ship disengaged from the dome at the top of the Stalk. It began to move slowly away from the planet, that grew smaller and smaller in their wake.

That had been home. That had been her life. That had been everything. Maybe she would go to her home planet, find her mom or her sister, wherever they had ended up. What else did she have?

As she watched, the planet below began to shake and rumble; the Stalk vibrated and swung back and forth, until it was sucked down, smaller and smaller, vanishing into the core of the planet. The next moment, everything turned into a fuzzy brown haze as the planet condensed in on itself. The ship rumbled as the wave of energy from the planet's implosion rocked them.

"It's gone," Jack breathed.

Goodbye, she heard, though the voice was very small, very far away. *Don't forget about me.*

I won't, she thought back.

The ship slowly turned, the remains of the planet disappearing from view until all she could see was the blackness of space.

How to Abduct an Alien

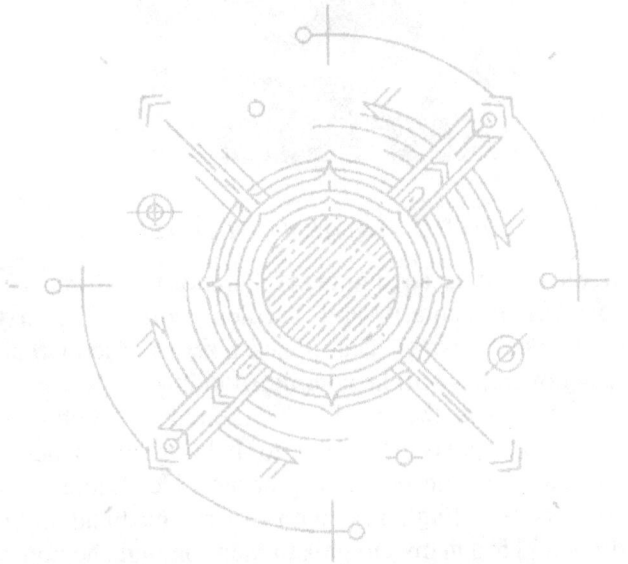

CAMERON J. QUINN

CAMERON J. QUINN

How to Abduct an Alien

Cameron Quinn is an author of Paranormal Romance, Horror, Urban Fantasy, and Thriller genres. The first season of The Starsboro Chronicles, a series of ten Urban Fantasy novelettes will be completed in 2017.

She works as the Head of Marketing at Amphibian Press; a small press dedicated to helping independent authors navigate the publishing ocean. Her home is in central New England with her husband, three children, and too many animals to mention, but she hopes to travel a bit before truly settling down.

She can be found on her website as well as Facebook, Twitter, Goodreads, and Instagram.

www.cameronquinnbooks.com

How to Abduct an Alien

CAMERON J. QUINN

Zurik stared at the reflection of a sliver of the moon on the placid water of the local swimming hole. He briefly wondered how often they checked it for gators as he took another swig of Jack Daniel's whiskey. The sickly sweet alcohol burned his throat on it's way down to hurting his empty stomach.

"You actually showed up!" Trent's disbelief would have angered him two months ago. But since Sianna passed away he couldn't find it in him to care. His girlfriend of two years was dead at just 17 years old and it was his fault. Since then, Zurik found it hard to care about much of anything. His heart hurt and the whiskey wasn't cutting it anymore. When Trent asked Zurik to meet him here he figured the distraction might help.

"Yeah," Zurik said looking at he half empty bottle. "Mind telling me why I'm here?"

"You know Stanley," Trent gestured to the kid standing next to him. Stanley was small and thin as a rail. He could usually be found under some bully's boot heel.

Zurik nodded. "He saw something the other day and no one believes him. I thought we could help."

"Yep, the Scooby Gang is at your service," Zurik looked up. The stars shone in varying brightness that twinkled in the midnight blue of the almost moonless sky.

"Ah, well—I was out here star gazing and I saw what happened to Janie Wright."

Zurik sobered and looked at Stanley with renewed interest. Janie was Sianna's best friend, everyone assumed she'd run off after her friend's death and some even accused the girl of being involved. Zurik knew that couldn't be the case, but had little evidence.

"What did you see?"

"Well, she was down here by the water, with her boyfriend, Jack. They were—you know," he flailed his arms as he struggled with the words.

"They were fooling around?" Zurik offered as he took a deep breath to calm his irritation.

"Yeah." Stanley said. "And then this large ball of light—"

"Hold up," Zurik said with a laugh. "Are you saying she was abducted by aliens?"

"Well, I don't know who was in the ship but that's probably a good—"

"Trent, why did you call me out here?"

"I thought we could—"

"No, this is crazy. If aliens were traveling to earth do you really think they'd be taking people?"

"Well actually we do it to animals all the time to study them so yeah I—" Trent argued.

"Well, you got the wrong guy." Zurik started passed them. "If you see E.T. tell him to phone home for me."

"You're an elf hybrid from another dimension, who hunts demons and monsters in his spare time! Why is it so hard to believe that aliens exist?"

"Zurik wait!" Trent called. "Look!"

Zurik kept walking. He felt dizzy and disoriented and looked at the bottle of Jack. Light flooded the small area around him. He dropped the bottle and watched it fall to the earth far below him.

"What the f—." Everything went black.

Zurik woke up in the dark with sounds of large pistons firing and moving metal all around him. A weight on his chest made it hard to breath and he was strapped to some kind of table. He squinted in the darkness. There was a door or opening of some kind in the wall to his right. He moved to sit up and pain lanced through his torso. He pulled his arms free of the straps and placed his hands on the large metal disc on his chest. He pushed it up and felt tubes and wire pulling free of his skin and muscles.

He let out a guttural yell as he threw the disc to the floor. Blood poured from his chest as he stood up. The pain pulsed through his torso but he needed to get out of here. He stood and made his way to the door. His legs were unsteady beneath him so he braced himself on the wall as he continued forward.

The ship was dark and cold as he passed through winding corridors. The sound of footsteps bounced off the walls towards him. He slipped into an open doorway and hid behind a large cylinder that went from the floor to the ceiling. The steps paused outside the door for a moment and two shadows appeared on the floor through the doorway. Zurik held his breath and pressed against the cylinder for what felt like forever.

When they left he took a deep breath and slid into a seated position, resting against the cold metal. His eyes adjusted to the dim lighting of the room and he noticed more cylinders a few feet apart, spanning the length of the room. He walked over to one and placed his hand on it. A blue light flashed on inside. There in the cylinder with tubes up her nose and in her mouth and her eyes closed as if she were sleeping, he found Janie Wright.

Zurik took a step back inspecting the cylinder for a latch, a plug, anything that might tell him how to get her out of here. The footsteps sounded again. They were too close. He turned and saw three creatures staring at him through huge black eyes. Their grey green skin seemed to blend in with the darkness and their expressionless faces sent a feeling of unease through him.

One of them pointed into the hallway. Zurik didn't move. It pointed at him and then into the hallway.

Zurik shook his head.

The creature seemed to sigh before leaving the room. A moment later a larger creature entered. It had sharp teeth and hunched over like a tiger stalking it's prey. Zurik pulled his gun out of his waist band and opened fire. He got a few rounds off before the small creature entered the room again and shot him with a taser-style projectile. He hit the deck and was unable to move as electricity pulsed through his veins.

Zurik woke up to the chill of cold metal on his skin and something pulling at his chest and stomach. Zurik squinted up, trying to see who was touching him through the bright white lights. He went to lift his hand only to find it was strapped to the table. He looked at the restraints, they used twice as many this time. There were a few creatures standing over him. One of them pointed at him and looked at the one across the table. As Zurik's eyes adjusted he saw a third entering the room with a cup and a strange metal rod in its hand.

"You're not probing me," he said as he pulled on the straps. They didn't budge. The beings started to rush around, one grabbed his arm to hold him still. He pulled the other arm with everything he had. He heard the distinct sound of the fiber giving way and pulled harder. It snapped and he slammed his fist into the one that was holding him. The blow sent the creature flying back into a table. Tools skittered across the floor as each of the creatures began whooping and screaming. Zurik ripped the rest of the straps and hopped off the table. He looked around for his clothes but the threat of the larger creature showing up while he didn't have a weapon made him give up.

He ran out into the hallway. Both directions looked the same, exactly like every other part of the this hell hole. Footsteps could be heard coming form the right so he ran left. Ducking into a small opening and hiding in the shadows. The large creature walked down the hall, barking orders at the smaller ones. When they'd left he snuck back out into the hall.

Go right.

Zurik looked around the ship for the source of the voice.

Trust me.

Zurik started to go left.

I want to help. You can save the girl and get home safely if you just listen to me.

"Who are you?" Zurik asked folding his arms over his chest.

I'm an alien, at least to you. I'm an anthropologist if you will. Go right. Do it now or you're going to get caught again and next time they'll use metal to hold to you to the table.

Zurik went right slowly.

Run!

He broke into a jog and then a run. Carefully placing his feet to remain silent as he moved through the ship.

There will be a corridor on your left, take it.... NOW.

Zurik came to a door way with a touch screen combination lock. The symbols on the lock were unlike anything he'd ever seen. He threw his hands up in frustration and the door opened.

Zurik went through a doorway. This part of the ship looked more like something from an episode of Star Trek.

Slow down.

Zurik slowed looking in windows. There were various animals in cages to the back to the first room. They were all asleep and the tables were empty. Each table had a bunch of medical style instruments on it.

"Is this a research... ship?"

Yes. We're part of a group sent to study your planet. Earth to you or Planet 1679, as we call it. Keep moving or you'll get caught.

Zurik started walking. Hoping the movement might quell the panic building in his chest.

The girl you were with earlier is in a room to your right in about fifty paces. I'm here as well so please don't panic when you see me.

"Is she awake?"

Nearly. It'll go better if you're here when she regains consciousness.

"Do you have my clothes?"

I grabbed something you should be able to wear. I don't know much about earth clothing. You're all so different in shape and size.

Zurik turned the corner and entered the room. The alien he assumed was the one communicating with him stood next to a table with his arm outstretched. A pair of grey sweatpants were in his four fingered hand. Zurik put the sweats on and then looked at Janie. She lay sound asleep. Her tight black curls splayed around her head and her flawless brown skin made her look almost peaceful.

Her eyes started to move behind her lids and her arms and legs twitched. She launched herself upright as her eyes opened.

Janie woke with a start. Her eyelids were heavy and she had to fight to open them. Her heart raced as she tried to find something familiar. Her dreams were so vivid. Nightmares like nothing she'd never experienced before. The pain was so real. Her body still ached. Her hand hit the cool metal of the table and panic crept up her throat as she began to hyper ventilate.

Warm hands gripped her shoulders and she screamed as she swung her arm back.

"Shhh," the deep male voice sounded familiar and— scared? "You're alright, Janie."

She forced her eyes open to see Zurik D'Vordi's electric blue eyes staring right into her soul.

"Where are we?" her voice quivered with the question. She didn't really want to know.

You're on the Intergalactic 51, mission: study planet 1679 and its creatures.

Janie turned slowly looking for the source of the voice. Something about it was off. Like it was actually part of her thoughts. Zurik grabbed her chin and pulled her back to look at him.

"Before you look over there, I need you to trust me," Zurik gave her a smile that didn't even get close to reaching his eyes. He wasn't sure this was the right thing. But with what she knew about Zurik it must be their only shot. Zurik's eyes moved from her to somewhere over her shoulder. She followed his gaze to a strange creature. It had huge black eyes and grey skin. It held its own hand and shuffled around.

"He's going to help us get back home."

"And there's no other way?" she asked as flashes of creatures that looked just like him hurting her under a blinding white light flew through her mind. Her panic rose again. Threatening to escape in the form of tears.

"He's not the scariest thing here," Zurik said. She'd never heard him like this. Unsure of himself.

She nodded and hopped off the table. Zurik wore a pair of grey sweats and clutched a glock .45 in his hands. His feet were bare and he had some wound on his stomach and what looked like small bullet holes all over his chest.

"You escaped the table."

"We can talk about everything and cry it out later when we are home," his voice transformed. It wasn't nervous anymore, it was determined.

I'll call them in, you will hold the gun to my head and order they send all three of us to the planet's surface, where you were taken from. Then you'll tell them they can come back and get me in three days time. At which point you will discuss their further activities on Earth.

"OK," Zurik nodded. "I can do this. Janie stay behind me."

Zurik wrapped an arm around the alien's torso and held the gun to his head. He let out a loud whistle and foot steps approached. Janie pushed her panic back with deep breaths as she latched onto Zurik's arm. She bounced back and fourth on the balls of her feet fighting the urge to run as the footsteps got louder and louder. Zurik shifted his weight as if her nervousness were seeping into him. Or his seeped into her. She really wasn't sure.

The group of alien beings entered the room. Each had a long cylindrical weapon. There were four of the creatures. And she couldn't help but remember Zurik's comment about the scarier things on this ship as she looked around them into the dark shadows of the ship.

"Alright assholes!" Zurik shouted. The alien he was pointing the gun at started making clicking and ticking sounds. Fear shot through Janie as he continued to speak. Her breathing sped up and the edges of her vision began going dark. The alien stopped and Zurik seemed as frozen as she felt. "I don't remember what the fuck I was going to say."

The alien started clicking and ticking again and the others lowered their weapons. They looked at each other for a moment and stepped back leaving an opening through to the door.

Go now, I'll lead you.

"Through there?" Janie asked. Her voice a squeak as fear seized her throat.

"We can do this," Zurik said. His determination returning. They moved forward with the gun still aimed at the alien. He directed them down the hallway towards a room with a large glowing white disc in the center.

This is going to feel strange. People are usually unconscious for this part.

The floor lit up covering them in a bright white light. Janie clutched Zurik's arm with all she had as she squeezed her eyes shut. They were lifted up off the floor and then they were falling. Janie buried her face in Zurik's shoulder as her stomach leapt into her chest and then dropped. Her feet hit the ground and she looked around to see the make-out spot she'd been at with her boyfriend earlier. The cool night air was moist and made her feel instantly sticky. The sounds of frogs and insects was deafening.

"Holy fuck," Zurik took a few steps away. Janie stepped forward, pain tripping through her guts. She and Zurik both leaned forward and the contents of their stomachs splashed on the dirt between them. Janie took a few steps back and fell to her knees. Reveling in the feel of the earth beneath her.

Zurik straightened and wiped his mouth. He started chuckling and it morphed into a full blown laughing fit.

"What's so funny?" Janie laughed the words as relief flooded her body.

"Thanks for puking with me, very classy of you not to let me puke alone."

"I do my best." She laughed. "How did you get on the ship? How did I get on the ship? How do I make sure I never get on a ship again?"

That's part of why I wanted to come here. We don't treat you with any kind of decency or respect and I'd like to change that. I have some pull and I think I can really bring change and end human abductions. I just need more evidence.

"Evidence of what?" Janie asked.

"That humans are intelligent beings and are capable of a higher understanding."

Janie and Zurik exchanged a look.

"Let's get out of here," Zurik started down the path toward the parking area. "I don't know about you but I need a drink."

"Tequila?" she asked feeling hopeful.

"I can manage that." Zurik laughed.

Zurik watched the sky as they made their way to the woods. The path was clear through the undergrowth. Zurik sent a silent prayer that Trent left his car behind.

After a few minutes they reached the small dirt parking area and sure enough his red 1969 Camaro with white racing stripes was still there. It had rust around the wheel wells and needed a new coat of paint but he was fixing it slowly.

"Thank god!" he said as he flopped onto the hood. "Baby, I missed you."

This is the mode of transportation? The disgust in the alien's voice was evident

"I'll ignore your tone," Zurik snapped.

"Most of us drive things that aren't so... old." Janie offered.

"Zurik!" Trent's voice came from the back seat as a shadow moved through the car and his face appeared in the driver's seat.

"Dude," Zurik laughed. "Why are you sleeping in my car?"

"You've been gone two days. I wasn't sure when they'd drop you back here or if they'd drop you back here. But I couldn't go home without you."

"Why not?"

"Grandpa would kill me and if he didn't, you know Lex would." Their uncle did have a murderous streak but rarely where they were concerned.

"Days?"

"Yeah, this is night three." Trent stepped out of the car. And smiled at Janie. "Oh good, you found her."

"Yeah," Zurik gestured to the alien. "This is... you never told us your name."

You couldn't pronounce it.

"OK, what should we call you then?"

I don't understand the human naming system.

"Just call him Tim and lets move on," Janie snapped. "I want to get home. I need a roof over my head like ten minutes ago."

"Alright," Zurik gestured to the drivers side door. "The other door doesn't open."

They all climbed in and the engine roared to life with a flick of his wrist. He put it in reverse and backed down the path toward the main road.

"So what are we supposed to do with Tim?" Trent asked after a few minutes of silence.

I need to observe humans in their natural environment.

"So you can take him to the mall," Zurik laughed. "And maybe the university?"

"Maybe we could get Gramps to take him to the office?" Trent asked.

"Doubtful."

I really don't need a guide, I can manage.

"No you can't," they said in unison.

"You know, I don't think I'm ready to go home."

Zurik looked over to Janie who was peering out the window at the sky.

"You can stay with us tonight, but you're parents are worried about you Janie. We can't put it off too long."

"I understand. I just don't know what to tell them yet."

The car fell silent. What could any of them tell anyone?

When they pulled up to their grandfather's large country style home, Lex's Harley sat in the driveway.

"At least we can get it all over with at once..." Trent's attempt to see the bright side caused a tick to start in Zurik's jaw. He just wanted to sleep in the safety of his own bed.

Markus ran out of the house. His hair was just beginning to show signs of aging and turn grey above his ears. He had fine lines around his green eyes.

Lex was right behind him. The fear left his eyes as soon as he saw the two boys and was replaced by anger.

"Where the hell have you been?" he snarled as Markus embraced his grandsons.

"Good question," Zurik snapped then turned to Tim who was still sitting in the car.

"Thank the Gods you two are alright. And is that, Janie Wright?" Markus said as he pulled her into a hug as well. "Everyone feared the worst, Janie. You've been missing for a little over a week"

"What is that?" Lex asked following Zurik's gaze.

"That's Tim," Zurik said with a nonchalance he didn't feel. He just wanted Tim to go home and never see him again.

"OK, what is Tim?"

"An alien," Zurik said as he pushed past his uncle to enter the house. "Duh."

"You little shit, get back here."

"Lex, he's obviously been through something, give the kid a minute." Markus's tone wasn't asking.

"I can tell you what I know," Trent offered. "And Tim can fill in the blanks. Come on Tim!"

Zurik sat in the window with one leg hanging outside. The patio and pool were just below before the rolling green forests that made up the backyard. His grandfather had made it big in the business world shortly after arriving in this dimension. While Zurik didn't know much about life in Ma Bet he'd learned his grandfather's part in a huge war and that he was considered one of the worst Kings in the land's history. Zurik had heard Lex and Markus arguing about his and Trent's upbringing which quickly diverged into name calling and Zurik learning the truth about his grandfather.

He stared at the night sky, picking out constellations and wondering if shooting stars were even stars at all. He glanced over his shoulder at his bed as the door creaked and light spilled in from the hallway. Janie stood in the doorway clutching the frame and scanning the room for him. When her honey colored eyes landed on him she gave a small satisfied smile that didn't reach her eyes.

"There you are," she said pushing the door the rest of the way open. "Tim is learning about the finer aspects of fast-food. We got you a burger."

He gave a smile and put out his hand as she offered him the paper wrapped grease ball.

"Thanks," he unwrapped his food and she sat on the other side of the window.

"Doesn't it freak you out to be this close to the sky?" she asked as she wrapped her arms around herself.

"It freaks me out more if I can't see the sky."

She looked at it. Her face an unintentional grimace.

"What are the chances you're going to be able to sleep tonight?" Zurik asked.

"Nonexistent. You?"

"Same," Zurik said around a mouthful of burger. "Wanna play cards?"

"You read my mind."

Trent stood outside the corner store and watched as Tim eyed the coke in front of him.

"You drink it," Trent said stifling a laugh.

"It's moving."

"It's carbonated. It has bubbles."

"Why?"

"Human's like different textures."

"Fascinating. Our food is all liquid. Eating is necessary but there's little pleasure in it. Not like here. This is wonderful."

"Glad you're enjoying yourself. I figure we'll hit the university library next. You can brush up on human history from the human perspective."

"I'm curious to see the differences in your interpretations as well as what gaps exist in your knowledge of the time before the written word."

"I'm curious about that myself." Trent said. Zurik and Janie fell asleep as soon as the sun rose leaving Trent to help Tim get the most our of his visit to earth.

Trent gave a chuckle as he looked at Tim again. People were giving him a wide birth but the baseball cap, Hawaiian shirt and board shorts seemed to disguise him pretty well.

Tim took a tentative sip and sputtered as the bubbles wreaked havoc on his sinuses.

"I think I'll stick to burgers for now." Tim said as he pushed the coke away. Trent grabbed the bottle and tossed it into the trash.

Tim followed him the short walk up the road toward The University of Starsboro North Carolina.

Carson Renshaw ran a hand through his hair as he read the chemistry paper over the brim of his coffee cup. The stress of school was nothing compared to life at home. He thrived in this environment. He was built to run a lab of his very own. This was just a stepping stone to the life he deserved.

Voices approaching the open main doors broke his concentration. Carson looked up to see a high school kid, Trent, who studied here often with a... Carson closed his eyes and then looked back at Trent's companion. It appeared to be an alien in an incredibly poor disguise. Who wore Hawaiian shirts anymore?

"You need to be quiet in here," Trent was saying. "It's the rule and we don't want to draw unnecessary attention.

The alien turned toward Trent and made gesture with his hands.

"Yes," Trent said.

Telepathy. Fascinating.

Carson found himself following them toward the history section of the library. His chem paper abandoned on the table.

Janie stared at her front door. She heard voices inside and shrunk down in her seat, the leather squeaking as she wiggled out of view of the house's occupants.

"You have to go back eventually." Zurik said. He was irritated. Though that seemed to be his default since they'd gotten back so she doubted it was her doing.

"You're grandfather understands and knows weird shit happens and you were only gone for a few days. This part was easy for you."

"Well, I could leave you in a field somewhere and call it in. The cops could come find you and then you could fake amnesia."

"Really?" that sounded like a good plan.

"You'd need to stop drinking water so you'd be dehydrated to help sell the story."

"I can do that," she nodded. "But you need to call it in anonymously. There's no way my dad didn't notice this car."

"I'll introduce myself later as a concerned classmate."

He put the car in gear and drove away from her home. The relief that flooded her was strange. She'd always loved being home. Preferring to stay in with her family than go out to parties and other high school event. As the house drifted away, she hoped the next time she saw it she'd want to stay.

"Zurik?" her voice wavered as tears threatened to spill onto her cheeks. "Can we do it tomorrow?"

He looked at her for a long moment. Far longer than the driver should look at anything that isn't the road.

"Yeah."

She looked out the window so he couldn't see her tears and his phone jingled and he didn't hesitate to accept the call. She wiped her eyes, grateful for the interruption.

"You what?" he yelled into the phone. "How could you lose an alien? He's the only one on the freaking planet!"

She looked over at him as the seriousness of the situation hit her. The other's were expecting him back tomorrow night.

"It's you're problem Trent, call me when you find him."

"You know if we don't get him back, the others are going to come looking for him right?" the irritation in Janie's tone caused a tick to start in Zurik's jaw. "He's like alien royalty."

"What?" Zurik snapped. He would have helped an alien prince escape his ship to explore earth.

"He said his father runs the intergalactic space something or other and he's supposed to take over. That's why he's like an anthropologist. He's trying to understand the different life forms he's going to be in charge of."

"When did he say all this?"

"When you were sulking in your room."

"You want me to drop you off at home right now?"

She glared.

"My point is," she began. "They're going to expect him to be ready for pick up tomorrow night. I don't want to find out what happens if he isn't there. So, if you won't help, could you at least drop me off with Trent?"

Zurik glared at the road as if he could scare it into taking him to Tim's location. The only thing worse than going back on that ship would be having those things running around down here.

Without acknowledging it he turned onto University Lane and headed toward the library on campus,

Trent was pacing by the front door with a phone to his ear. He looked up and relief flooded his features as he recognized Zurik.

"Thank the gods," Trent said dropping the phone. "Lex in the middle of his fight, we're on our own."

"What happened?" Janie asked.

"He was reading about the second world war and Tim went to the bathroom and when he didn't come back I went to look for him but he was gone. The bathroom was a mess and there was no sign of him anywhere."

"Are you saying someone abducted our alien?" Zurik asked.

"I think so."

"Shit."

👽

Tim woke up to the feeling of cold metal underneath him. He was strapped down and it took his eyes a few minutes to clear. Blinking he looked around the room. He was surrounded by strange computers and charts. Something was beeping and another machine was whirring. A bright light obscured most of his vision but he could see a little to his right.

A man in a long white coat was looking over data on in front of one of the computers.

Where am I?

The man straightened and turned around. "Fascinating! Can you speak physically or only with your thoughts?"

You wouldn't be able to understand my language and it's difficult for me to pronounce yours with my mouth. Now, where am I?

"You're in my lab," the man smiled and Tim felt something he'd never felt before. It was a strange uneasiness just above his belly and he doubted it was from the earth food Trent gave him. No, this was something else. Something that told him to get out of there right now.

"I don't have time to argue with you. Get in the car, go back to my place and wait or I will put you in the car and dump you at your house, the choice is yours."

"You're an asshole, Zurik D'Vordi!" Janie yelled in his face as she snatched the keys from his hand.

"As long as you live through this, I can live with that."

She peeled out of the library parking lot and hopped the curb on her way to the main street. A hubcap rolled down the road after her.

"I'd say you handled that well, but I don't like to lie, its a slippery slope." Trent said as they watched the rusted red car disappear from view.

"You're the one who lost the alien."

"What happened to Sianna wasn't your fault." Trent argued.

"Yes, it was." Zurik snapped as he headed for the library. "If I hadn't shown her that world she would still be alive."

"You don't know that" Trent continued. "She could have been hit by a bus, or died of cancer. If there's one thing I've noticed about humans, it's that they don't let the fear of death stop them because they've already accepted their fate. It's different for us, we don't know if we're going to die of old age or even age beyond 25."

"Thanks for that, it's not like I'm not in the same boat as you and had the exact same upbringing or anything. Your point of view is so enlightening."

"Zurik—,"

"Trent," Zurik cut him off. "We have an alien to find before his psycho family pops in for an invasion. Shut up and help me get the security footage from the library."

👽

The security footage Trent was able to look over while

Zurik chatted up the librarian showed Tim being drugged with something like chloroform and dragged out of a fire exit by a student of the University. He wasn't liked by his peers by any means. In fact several believed he might be a psychopath. Luckily one of them had been to his lab before. It was just off campus in an old office building. It used to be bustling with businesses but since the economy took a dive a year or so ago, the building only held a cat bathing service and Carson's lab. Trent went around the back and Zurik crept passed the angry sounds of cats being bathed toward the front.

He slipped inside and closed the door. As soon as the latch clicked in, the muzzle of a small hand gun poked the back of his head.

"I figured you'd show up eventually. Whenever Trent has a problem you're never far behind."

"Well, what can I say," Zurik laughed. "That's what big brothers are for."

"I don't want to hurt you."

"You won't." Zurik turned around grabbing the gun and pulled down and into his hip he twisted it out of Carson's hands. Zurik tossed the gun to the side and Carson took out some kind of pepper spray bottle and the next thing Zurik knew he was on the floor unable to move.

"You're paralyzed temporarily," Carson explained as he dragged Zurik toward the table that help Tim. "You might hallucinate a bit as well. The side affects vary from person to person. Most women have complete memory loss as well. It's amazing the things you can find in fungus if you only think to look. Oh, don't worry it'll wear off in a few minutes. Just long enough for me to tie you up—or kill you—I haven't really thought about that part yet."

An alarm sounded and Carson dropped Zurik's leg.

"That'll be Trent in my trap." He giggled to himself. "He's very smart for a teenager, I'm a little surprised I caught him."

He left the room and Zurik was left with Tim. Zurik lay partially underneath the table. Tim's hand was hanging over the side, unmoving. Panic flooded Zurik's chest. He tried to speak to the alien but his words were nothing but a moan.

I don't have much time left. He's cut me open. I don't know how much longer I can last.

Carson dragged Trent in by his feet. His eyes were open but he wasn't able to move either.

Carson walked across the room to look at them. "I can't believe I pulled this off. I abducted an alien and then out smarted the D'Vordi brothers. You know I always knew I was smart but you guys are always getting in the way of anyone doing anything even just a little bit unethical around here," Carson said as he tied Trent's hands with thick rope. Then pulled Zurik the rest of the way to the back wall and tied him as well. "What I really want to know is, how you two got an extraterrestrial being in the first place."

Zurik looked to Trent's unconscious form next to

him. His panic turning to rage, it still wasn't enough to help break free of the flesh and blood prison. The tips of his fingers began to tingle and twitch.

"Look at this," Carson said as he stared into Tim's chest cavity. "Two hearts. I wonder if one is enough to keep him alive or if he needs both."

"You're going to kill him," Zurik slurred.

"Perhaps. But it's all in the name of science."

Zurik saw a shadow shoot across the lab, Carson was too busy to notice. His eyes reached behind the table. A mass of tight black curls crept along the back wall.

"His people will come looking for him," Zurik said drawing Carson's attention. The room began to spin and colors grew more intense. He blinked and shook his head to clear it.

"The hallucinations have started. Perfect. That should keep you busy until I'm done for the day at least."

Zurik fought to see straight and for a moment everything was clear. Then the walls began to move, and the table seemed to melt.

The sound of metal cracking a skull and the thud of a body hitting the floor filled the room. Zurik struggled to see what was happening. Janie stood over Carson's body with a monkey wrench in both hands. She dropped it and ran to Tim.

"What did he do to you?"

Nothing my people didn't do to you.

"How do I fix it?" she asked bouncing back and forth

on the balls of her feet in nervous anticipation.

Remove the chest spreader, my body will do the rest. Check if any knives or anything in my chest cavity first.

Janie leaned over him and looked into his wound. She reached in and gently removed a scalpel. Then she unlocked and removed the chest spreader. As Tim's chest closed itself Zurik began to get movement back. First in his fingers and toes.

"How did you know where to find us?" Zurik asked during a moment of clarity.

"GPS on your phone. You're grandfather tracks you and the password to his computer is Zurik&Trent."

"We have to get out of here." Trent said as he came to. He was pale and looked like he might vomit. "Do either of you see the weird little unicorn?"

He was grabbing at something invisible in front of his face.

"It's from the drug. Carson said it might cause hallucinations."

"It says its someone's imaginary friend." Trent said as he fell over and passed out.

"You brought my car right?" Zurik asked holding his hands up to be untied. "Oh shit."

"What?" Janie asked.

"I see the little fucker too."

Thank you for driving me here. My people will be here

soon.

Janie watched as Tim got out of the car. He was moving slowly, obviously sore from his experience but he'd healed up well so far. Much faster than a person would. She felt a hand on her own chest as she looked at his wounds. She looked down to see it was her own. She'd been ripped apart like that too. She wasn't sure if it was better not to remember anything. The fear of what might have happened, and what they might have planted inside her. Her own body felt foreign to her. Tim must feel the same way.

"Will you be alright, E.T.?" she asked.

He looked back at her and nodded. *I think I finally have the evidence I need to stop my people from abducting yours.*

"Thanks." It felt lame but she didn't know what else to say.

"What do you mean there's an evil Santa!" Zurik yelled from the back seat.

They looked back to see him flailing before flopping back down.

Do you think they'll be alright?

"I'll get them home, you just worry about you." Janie smiled. The light appeared over Tim. He waved goodbye as he was lifted back into the ship. Once the craft was gone she started the engine and headed back toward the D'Vordi residence.

"What the hell happened to me?" Zurik said as he

climbed into the front seat. He was rubbing his eyes and shaking his head.

"You were hit with some kind of hallucinogen."

"That was some trip."

"Trent's still in it."

"Bummer." He looked back at his brother who was whimpering. "What happened to psycho the science guy?"

"He bailed." She said. "I got you guys to the car and by the time I got back he was gone."

Carson handed the immigration official his new ID. That damn women told the cops he was the one who'd kidnapped her. Of course he was half way across the country before he saw his picture on the news while fueling up. A pit stop at the local pharmacy and a bad dye job later, Carson Renshaw was dead. But Dr. Van Riel already had an interview for a job in Toronto.

Dead-Switch

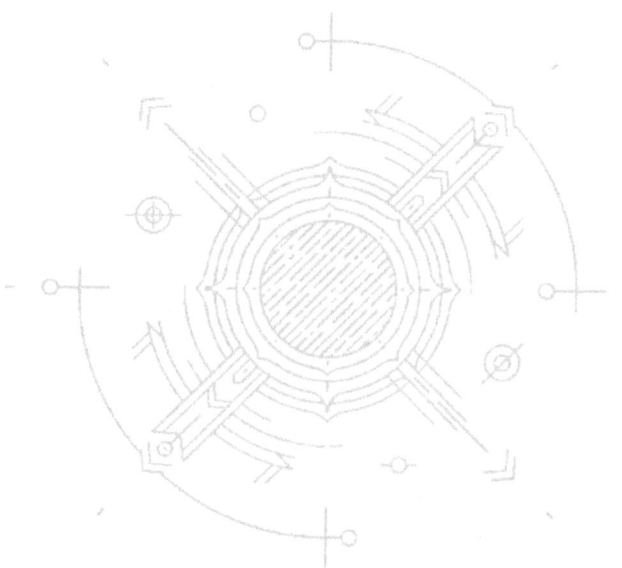

CULLEN MCHAEL

CULLEN MCHAEL

Dead-Switch

Cullen McHael dwells in the remote steppes of rural Iowa, where the stars burn holes in the endless boredom and crop circles carve themselves in rows of corn. Cullen began writing and producing film and television in 2005, joined a circus in 2006, kickboxed in Thailand in 2007, started producing documentary films for aid organizations in 2008 and has been teaching filmmaking and writing since 2010. Interests include futurism, fighting and mythology.

Past works include the webseries Wormtooth Nation, the feature film The Vindication of Ronald Clay, and the documentary Saving the Disposable Ones.

He can be found on his website and Facebook and Twitter.

Dead-Switch

CULLEN MCHAEL

Rainwater drips into a dumpster with a sound like an iron bell, welcoming me to the dead end of a blind alley on the wrong side of town. I've got an empty wallet, a stomach trying to eat my spine and a bounty on my head big enough to fund a whole hit squad's Havana vacation. But the real problem is the bomb between me and the answers to my problems. What do you do when you're a two finger grip from hitting bottom? You reach for a friend.

Perfume and vinegar drift on the rain-damp air, but from the garbage or the broken windows of the buildings around me, I don't know. That sweet smell blends with the vapors of kimchi from the Korean restaurant around the corner to make something just bordering on pleasant in a too-strong, make-your-eyes-water kind of way.

I tap a control on The Killer, my custom pistol, and a beam of UV light floods from its barrel. My goggles make the light visible so I can see where others wouldn't, but the alley still seems empty. It's not like her to be late.

Mismatched cat's eyes flash in the hidden light. In the shadows of the waste container someone crouches, watching me. It must be her, but cat's eyes? Those're new. I need my goggles to see the beam, but those eyes would have seen it coming before I rounded the corner. Maybe it's not her. My feet settle to a shooting stance.

"Killer at the ready, Maxine?" the shadow hisses, proving this is the cannibal I've come to see. "That any way to greet a friend?"

Her soprano voice is taught as a mandolin, but something in the tone tells me she's making a joke.

"It's Max," I remind her, again. "After that business in Hong-Kong, I couldn't be sure."

I don't holster The Killer, but I keep its light off of her. Where the beam falls on the brick of the alley-floor, it makes a rain-puddle shimmer in a way my goggles don't like. The puddle resolves as a gold and black haze of electronic snow. "Is Set around?"

"Was Hong-Kong our fault?" She spits. "Not how we remember it."

"Yeah. That'd be why I'm feeling cautious. Wasn't sure if you might be carrying a grudge. I guess Set's watching from somewhere up high?"

A couple of gunshots echo through the neighborhood and a cat yowls. Somewhere up above, a red-eye flight glides in low, carrying in strangers from distant lands. The wail of its engines wanders the brick and steel canyons.

"We split from Set." The cannibal's growl sounds like the rain-gutter got clogged. "If we carried a grudge for every fool we'd have hate for the whole world. If you worry, why come to us?"

"You know why, Jin," I deliberately holster the killer. "Because you're the best."

"Poppy-smoke." There's a hint of a smile hiding in that word, though she's still just a shadow at the alley's end. "We are all you have. Will you eat with us?"

The doors of the Korean restaurant open on a hive of tiny interconnected rooms separated by metallic gauze curtains. It's loud – loud with weird music like a flock of mechanical geese blasted from speakers that seem just out of sight around every corner, loud with sour and spice smells. The walls are undecorated brick and sections of corrugated steel painted garish colors. Jin settles at a table all the way in the back corner of a room barely larger than it. A rat squeaks among the hay strewn floor-boards as Jin circles the table three times. It's littered with food crumbs but she sits anyway.

To call it a dive might be a compliment, but it'll suit the purpose. The music should hide our conversation and despite passing through a few rooms before we sat down, I have no idea if there's anyone else in the building. If there is, I expect they're just as ignorant of us.

Jin waits to be served. When the waiter comes he delivers two plastic bowls full of fried rice covered in something goopy that's what I've been smelling. No menu. No how-do-you-do. Just two bowls and then he's gone. I guess this is what they're serving.

Jin tucks in, bending low over her bowl and eating with her fingers.

I let my goggles hang from my neck. The only light in the room points at the golden curtain over the door we came in by. That light bounces shimmering orange and gold reflections across the room not unlike firelight.

A single scoop of rice makes my mouth explode with peppery pain. It's like eating liquid glass with a vinegar aftertaste.

There's no water. The waiter didn't bring any. I clutch the table and breathe. Oxygen passing over my tongue fans the flames.

"Something wrong?" the cat eyes catch moving light. The bigger one's the color of healthy moss, the smaller burnished gold. Her black hair's been shorn very short and hangs in tufts. Her cheeks seem more gaunt than I remember, her skin a little paler. She didn't take off her gloves when she started eating.

"Cat eyes?" I wheeze. "That's new. Who's your cutter? It's good work."

"Jackson," she says, and goes for another scoop from her pain bowl. "So, job?"

"Jackson deals in secondhand parts." My stomach squirms.

"We all deal in second-hands and parts. That's why we are called cannibals." She studies me a moment, with a ball of rice goop sticking to her gloved fingers. "Except you. You only take new parts, yes? What is the job?"

"A safe-house. It'll have untraced identity papers, guns, emergency money, all the stuff a well-funded spy hidey-holes away for a rainy day. We split the take."

"How much money?"

"A few thousand."

"Security?" She goes back to shoveling rice.

"Standard stuff. It's a tenant building so nothing dangerous until we're inside the apartment, though I expect the lock's pretty good. The building's in citizen-land where the black-and-blues snoop wireless, so have to stay off the comms. There's a rent-a-guard but they won't know or care about the safe-house. Lots of foot traffic in the lobby so we should be able to waltz in. On the apartment door, a silent alarm rigged to notify the agency that built the place. Inside the house, probably trip wires, definitely a dead-man's code."

"Hmm…" She turns her head to stare at the glittering curtain and paws the air as if trying to brush aside the reflected light. "Dead-code – safe deposit box for the desperate. Tell us of this one."

"My source says it's a sink-5 rotary on a thirty second timer, hooked to about a pound of CL20 explosive.

Once the sensor's tripped you have thirty seconds to punch the correct code or it kills you with a boom."

"Have you got the code?"

"Maybe."

"Trust your source?"

"No." I pick a bit of rice out from under the pile where it might have less evil on it.

"A sink-5 we will hack in five seconds, if we can get beside it. But we wonder, maybe your source is the one from Hong-Kong and it is not a sink-5?"

"Like I said, I don't trust the source. That's why I need the best." I chew my way through the agony.

"What happened to him?"

"The Hong-Kong guy? No idea. I haven't been back."

"Hmm. Windows?"

"Seventh story of a twelve story building, no fire escape."

"But does the glass have a lock?"

"It's trivial to rig a glass-crack sensor to the silent alarm system, so let's assume that's what they've done."

She nods. Crows-feet at the corners of her eyes deepen as she thinks. The dancing light makes her pale skin a shifting red-gold and her lips black. The crows-feet are new. How long's it been since Hong-Kong? Two months? Three? I've packed a lot of trying hard not to die into those days. I guess she has too.

"Sorry about Set," I tell her. "Any particular reason she split?"

"Set did not like the company we keep," she says. "The sink-5, it has rumblers?"

"I don't know." I shrug, remembering Set's dour frown and ability to say nothing at all while still getting her point across. I was hoping if I hired Jin I'd get Set too, but I guess not.

"Sink-5 doesn't come with rumblers, but easy to make. If it doesn't, then we hack through the wall with an axe and a hammer, easy as milk. But if it does have rumblers, it picks up the shake as the wall breaks and we go boom." Those uneven eyes narrow as she wiggles her fingers.

"Yeah, I still don't know."

She wrinkles her nose and rubs some grease off her lips with the back of a gloved hand. "Then we not do that. Two systems, one for each of us. We will have double the normal rate for our part. Because of Hong-Kong."

"Rate? You're getting paid in take. I can give you two-thirds."

"Two-thirds take? Poppy-smoke." Her hands hover over her near-empty bowl, and the cat's eyes glitter in the shifting shadows. "We don't work on speck. Milk sours, we still get paid half."

"You used to work on speck," I tell her, remembering a dark alley not unlike the one we just met in, but in Nova Mundo and five years and a lot of bullets ago. "We used to do jobs like this all the time."

"We got better. Now we don't have to. We get paid. Like citizens." Her pupils are holes into a very deep cave. Her fingers curl around the edges of her bowl.

"I don't have any money, Jin. That's why I've got to do this. It's an easy job."

Her stare lingers through a whispering gap while the music switches songs. As a new rhythm starts, she says: "Very well. If we work on speck, then questions. If we don't like the answers, we will eat you for parts."

"Seems fair." My voice stays even, but my heart beats like a bruise. She wouldn't really. We've been close. It's just a figure of speech.

Forty minutes and forty lies later, we settle up and sneak out.

Lies to Jin aren't the best survival strategy. She's reliable, tough, competent and she knows her friends from her enemies. Despite her idiosyncrasies, her mind's sharp and her heart in the right place. Well, mostly. The work we've done together has had a way of turning sour, but that's not her fault. That's just the nature of my work. The thing is, if I told her the truth, she'd never agree to do this.

But if I don't get this done I'm dead, and if she doesn't help me, then I don't know what I'll do.

So I tell my lies and we make our plan, synch our watches and go our own ways.

Then it's 3 am and I stand with rain dripping down my neck, looking up at the twelve-stories of concrete and steel that house peasants, prostitutes, pimps, pushers and a safe-house that used to be mine.

The Inquisition built it for me, for if I ever had to burn my cover and disappear. I never expected the Inquisition would turn around and burn me, but everything changed in Hong-Kong.

So here I am, getting wet on a concrete-road between concrete monoliths with chimneys that push steam into a sky too thick with wet to hold it. My goggles whirr as they try to keep up with all the water and fail, turning everything to black and gold snow. They're near useless out here in the rain. The Killer sits on my hip like a lover's hand.

I need the money. I haven't got any. I need the guns. Life's hard. More than anything, I need the identity papers, because one of them is me. Not Max, the cover I've worn for years, but the real me, the original. The Inquisition will have destroyed whatever files they had of mine when they threw me from a loft balcony in Hong-Kong with two bullets in my chest, but they might not have known I made a copy of my original identity, including my commission as a covert officer. They might not know I put it under the floorboards of the safe-house they built me.

I haven't seen those precious files in ten years, since long before I met Jin. I barely know the person they describe, who I used to be. With the Agency out for me, my cover is my life now – Maxine the killer – a life of moving corpses for second-hand parts. I'm a black-market cannibal, just like all the friends I have left. I could destroy those papers, set off the Sink-5 and walk away, but then there would be nothing left of the street-rat from Bejaia, where no-one remembers my name. I haven't been back to that city since the Inquisition recruited me, and I may never go, but despite everything it remains the place that I am from. I'm not ready to surrender that. Not while everything in my life is a lie. But if any of my current friends or the surgeons they trade with find those papers, they'll find the Inquisition's stamp all over them, and that'll be the end of Maxine the Killer, and the end of the last of my friendships.

Like Jin.

So lying to Jin may not be the best strategy, but I've been lying for years, and the pile of lies is deep enough I might just be able to hide at its bottom. I'll make a new life out of the muck and loose parts. Maybe in time it will be real.

Because I'm not a mole anymore. Our jobs won't go mysteriously sour anymore. When I answer to the name Max, it won't be a lie anymore.

With some time we'll make a team. We'll do the work. Someday, if there's enough trust, maybe I even share some of what I once was, if only so we can find a way to put some hurt back on the clock-hearts who burned me. It'll be the tops. But it all starts here. An easy job will lead to more. Have to build trust. Have to be Maxine the Killer, now and hereafter.

Jin stands next to me. For how long, I'm not sure. Her black leather reflects a little of the street-lamp half a block past her. She smells like talcum and her skin looks dry.

"It rains," she says. "Why do you wait?"

"You," I tell her, and start toward the door.

Rows of locked post-boxes line the entry, which splits around a plastic cage holding the front desk. Inside that cage, the guard has his feet up, watching an air-race on his security monitor. The light plays on the ceiling like we're underwater. The race looks to be the Celtaen Lights – I didn't realize it was that time of year already. The guard's in his twenties and easy to look at – dark scruff lines a sharp jaw, big muscles and hair dyed luminous green so it makes the shoulders of his white guard-shirt glow. A couple of flower-eaters sit on the benches by the elevator, wearing the knitted patchworks of mechanicals and steeping in a haze from their long pipes. The elevator doors rattle closed on a bouquet of ladies in black leather corsets and too much makeup.

The guard looks up from the race as we approach.

"G'evening, Ladies," he says, with more cheer than is necessary and a white-toothed grin. The grin looks like the key to many a girl's puzzle, but his eyes are flat.

Shame. I was hoping we wouldn't be noticed or remembered.

I take Jin's hand and give him the middle finger. He blinks, throws the bird back, and then returns to staring at his box.

"Gotta sign in," he tells us, pointing at the screen outside his cage.

We go to the guest terminal and stand in front of it while he turns back to the race. A bearded crazy wanders in the door, on a course like he's tacking against a strong wind and muttering curse-words under his breath. He passes the guard unchallenged and stops to wait at the elevator. His new shoes have a bloodstain near the heel.

Jin and I turn our backs on the guard and head for the lift. The buttons have seen a lot of use – plastic circles with faded numbers in a steel plate polished by hand-grease. Jin shoos the crazy away with a steady look and a hint of bared teeth. He stares at his feet as he stumbles off, continuing his muttering about the world's end and heaven's wrath.

Maybe, buddy, but if heaven's got any wrath left for this world I surely haven't seen it.

My neck feels naked.

There's something odd about Jin's hand. Her knuckles are too hard, the bones too angular. Jin hadn't ever changed her hands before. They were original. Maybe it's not just the eyes that are new. But that's a lot of trade worth of parts. In three months? She wasn't kidding when she said she was doing well.

When the doors have closed on the lobby she drops my hand.

Bangs and clanks accompany our ascent. The lift sways on its cables. Dripping water patters against the roof. Smells like rust.

"You lost the pony-tail," Jin says. "You had grown it, what, ten years?"

"You remember the goon with the clamp hand in Hong-Kong?"

"Did not forget. His name was Vice." Her lips curl with smug humor.

"I thought it was Vick, with a hard c. Anyway he caught up with me in Moscow. Grabbed ahold of my hair while hanging off the back of a taxi."

She grimaces. "Hair handle. Easy to catch."

"That was about two seconds before he died."

She frowns. "But he took your hair."

As the floor gets close I draw The Killer to check its charge. Still as full as I left it. That's my boy – no leaks here. Five shots or five hours of light, which-ever comes first. The recharger cell clipped to my belt is one third empty. It'll give me maybe two and a half shots more, but that's the bottom of the barrel until we get inside the safehouse for more.

Jin watches my hands with a frown. "You kept the murderer."

"Couldn't live without it."

The elevator bell rings and a light shines behind the number 16 on the floor-o-meter. The numbers on my watch say go time.

"Clock-check. Two, one, mark," I chant, and start my stopwatch as she does the same. "Stay off the waves. See you in ten."

"We liked the hair-handle," she says as the elevator door tries arthritically to close between us. "Was brave to wear a hook."

Then she and the elevator are gone — banging away up the shaft toward the roof and her part of the job. The door keeps trying to close, but can't quite do it.

The hall's been redecorated. I remember drywall and hotel carpets. I've taken a dozen steps before I realize I'm wrong, it hasn't been redecorated. It's the same but older. The dry-wall's melted off the support beams and makes a chalky-white jigsaw puzzle on the floor. The level above must be flooded, because the paint and most of the ceiling blister with big dimples that trickle water. The mighty smell of mildew rushes my face in waves. Floorboards creak under my feet.

If my safe-house got flooded the papers will be gone and the money worthless. My stomach churns like a chimney-fire. I taste evil curry from Jin's restaurant. Water runs down the wall. I'm pretty sure the safe was water-proof.

The hall leads around a corner and past a dozen empty-looking apartments. The door that once was mine waits third to last, but I stop short of it by a dozen yards. Jin will be reaching the roof right about now. She was confidant she could get to the window. She wouldn't tell me how.

The hall smells abandoned – musty, mildew and drywall dust. I approach the door to the safe-house and examine the browning plastic of the residential lock system. Funny thing, memory. This code I remember. The one for the Sink-5, I do not. Forgetting that one little thing has made this into a whole job, but I don't mind – it's a job I get to do with Jin, and I'd have needed to do that anyway. The plastic cover over the keypad falls off instead of open, but the device inside accepts my code with a chirp and the "locked" icon changes to a "thumbs up." The glass-crack sensors should be offline now. I stand back to wait. There's no point going through the door until Jin signals the Sink-5's been disarmed.

I don't really know why she insisted on using the window. She can be a little weird. Maybe she calls herself "we" to acknowledge all the second hand parts. The thought sends a shudder down my throat.

The back of my neck itches. I feel exposed, standing in the hall.

The door to the apartment next to mine has a little drywall dust on its knob. It would have rubbed off if the door were in use. Lucky. From the window next-door I can watch Jin work. It'll make waiting a little less boring, and if she can't get in, I'll tease her and use the front door. Besides, I'll feel safer waiting in an abandoned apartment than out here in the hall.

My first kick knocks dust from the door-frame. My second splinters the latch seating and the door swings in on creaking hinges.

The apartment has the same layout as my safehouse next-door, but mirrored. Cheap carpet, bedroom on the right just inside the door, then the living-room with windows opposite the entrance, a little kitchenette huddled up under the windowsill, and a row of big windows. The floor's littered with drywall and bird poop. A breeze blows past me into the room, brushing musty fingers across my neck. One of the windows hangs open.

My goggles turn the shadows to gold, and then those shadows draw back like a tide as the device fills in detail. Dust and droppings crunch under my feet as I approach the window. Jin could have gone out this way - it's probably easier than the roof, but we didn't know it was here. I assumed these apartments would have people in them. It would be half hilarious to surprise her.

I've stopped by the open window. The breeze blows past me out it, pushing gently toward that open space and the long drop outside. Bird poop litters the sill. A raven, perched there, turns to look at me.

Fallen drywall crunches in the hall behind me. Like a footfall.

I draw the Killer and spin.

The door's open. Did I leave it open? An instant later, the steady breeze catches it and slams it shut, knocking dust off the ceiling and blowing puffs along the floor. No other movement.

I flick on the gun's light and UV, invisible to the human eye, floods the room. My goggles show me countless details in the concrete walls that peek out from behind fallen drywall, in the dust hanging in the air, in the piles of bird dung. A glimmer of residual heat fades on the doorknob. I didn't touch the doorknob.

Someone's following me.

I wait. If they're outside they'll have to open the door to get in. If they're in here, they must have ducked into the bedroom just as I spun around. Either way, I've got a clear firing line on their next move.

Minutes creep by. My breath whispers in my ears and my armpits sting with sweat. I lower the weapon to my hip, but keep it pointed down the hall.

The raven on the windowsill takes off like a good idea.

From outside the window comes the sound of a snake slithering. Rope? Jin. A tap must be the sound of her feet hitting the windowsill.

Another minute passes. The Killer will cook flesh but it might not burn through the bedroom wall. Even if it does, I've only got five shots. Better to wait. He'll show himself. Unless he's already called for backup. Stopwatch says it's been six minutes.

A scraping from outside sounds like a glass-cutter.

Come-on, bedroom guy. Show your face so I can fry you. The heist is happening.

But he doesn't.

The window to the safehouse opens with a couple of quiet clunks. A chirp, barely heard, is the Sink-5 saying its 30 second timer is counting down. Silence falls again.

Stopwatch says it's been seven minutes.

Deep breath. Time to move this along. I point my gun at the doorframe and pull the trigger. My goggles mute the flash. A hole opens in the wall, and smoke streams from it. I poke a second one.

"I can keep shooting all day," I lie. "Or you can surrender."

He steps around the doorframe with his hands in the air. Tall, broad-shouldered and narrow-hipped – my goggles aren't great for his features, making him a shimmering silhouette in the haze of smoke.

"Well, here we are," he says.

By his voice, it's the guard from downstairs. But that doesn't work. There isn't another lift and he got here less than a minute after I did. Sixteen flights of stairs in a minute? Maybe with the right set of legs.

"I guess you got me," he tries again. "What're you going to do?"

I flick my goggles and gun over to visible light. Sharp jaw, dark scruff, dead eyes. Same guy. Or there's a printing press rolling out hunky security officers somewhere. His hair isn't glowing anymore. It must have a switch.

As soon as my finger touches the control on the goggles, he moves. His left hand whips something small my way in the same instant he throws himself sideways into the living-room.

I pull the trigger and the killer lights the room like a pencil-thin crack into the heart of the sun. His dodge is elegant, well trained. Whatever he threw punches my left shoulder just under my collarbone, but The Killer's beam nails him square in the chest. Vapor explodes from his body, carrying the stink of seared meat. He hits the ground and doesn't move.

The thing he threw at me is a knife, buried about an inch between my top two ribs and sticking out like an old tombstone. It doesn't hurt yet.

Something in his chest cavity hisses like a cracked steam-valve and a septic smell joins the bouquet.

I pull the knife out. Blood trickles but doesn't spurt. It starts to sting. I sink a little deeper in the sea of suck. My left arm works fine, but I can feel the skin folding open like a wallet, and that shoots pain through me and blood down my chest. I'm out of bandages. That's how low things have gotten. It's a real bad idea to go on a job without bandages handy. From my pocket I pull my handkerchief, fold it, and tuck it under my bra-strap.

The pain buzzes across my shoulders as I walk past the corpse and out into the hallway. The recharger clips onto the Killer and starts to purr. Stopwatch says that took 15 seconds. Jin will be done with the Sink-5 if her boast was good.

As I look up from my watch, I come face to face with the security guy from downstairs. He's standing in the hall, hair shining blue, one eyebrow arched and a baton in his left hand. Behind him, the elevator doors stand open as the elevator sinks out of sight.

I look over my shoulder, back into the empty apartment, but no, it still smells of cooked meat and I can see the other guy's foot right where I left it. Somebody really must be maken'em on a press.

When I've turned back to the hall, he's swinging the club at my face.

I try to move but the baton skips off the top of my head, making blue and purple fireworks explode in my eyes. My knees buckle as his fingers close on my jacket-front. The Killer leaps to my hand but he pushes it aside with his baton and my bolt only serves to sear a black scar on the wall. Then the baton flicks and my wrist pops. The Killer spins across the floor and the recharger bounces free of it.

I'm airborne. He's lifting me with one hand – then I'm slammed against the wall and the wind rushes from me. Holding me still with that big hand, he turns to look over his shoulder and through the door I just came out of. He smells like a mandarin orange, and something else... Old Spice?

"Harold?" He calls. "You alright?"

"Nope," I wheeze, and jam my left thumb into his eye. My right hand's a tangle of pain.

He grunts and twists his face away but doesn't let go. I block his baton with my right forearm before it can hit my head again, and the impact jars what are definitely broken bones. His eyeball squeezes under my thumb and a wordless yell that's half animal escapes his lips. He bites my wrist. Skin and tendons pinch. His baton rails against my guarding arm. His teeth tighten, blood flows. Then his eyeball bursts.

He drops me and staggers back. The floor pounds my hip and shoulder and my knife-wound flashes agony. I roll onto my stomach and throw myself toward where The Killer waits in a pile of dust. My right arm gives out under me with a sliding pop and a sense of tearing. My fingers fall short of the killer's grip. The sea of suck is wide and deep.

"You shot Harold," he rants, "You shot my brother."

He's wearing wing-tips. They look expensive. Really nice shoes. One of them smacks into my ribs like a ball-peen hammer. I fall onto my right side as muscles in my gut cramp from the blow.

His knuckles smack my cheek-bone and fallen plaster presses a pattern into the other half of my face. It tastes like bitter chalk. I drag myself another arm's length along the floor, but his hands catch the strap of my goggles to snap my neck back. The killer's just another yard away. He wrenches my face around to look at him.

His hair's turned red. It changes with his mood? Lame peacockery. I liked the other brother better.

"To hell with the bounty. You hurt my brother," he growls. "I only have one brother."

"Had," I correct.

His other eye just about pops out of his head it goes so wide. "You killed him!"

"You took the wrong job."

His lips peel back from white teeth and he shifts his knee so he's straddling my chest. I can't wrestle with a broken wrist, so the best I can manage is to bring both forearms up to protect my face. He starts pounding. Deep breaths. I'm under-water now, and the deeps are sucking at me. Just have to doggy-paddle a few seconds. Something will change. Just have to hold on, keep breathing.

A left hook reaches around my guard and jogs my brain. Black dots swim. He grabs my right wrist. The bones shift.

Then the safe-house explodes.

The concussion hits like an elephant sitting on my head, and then just as suddenly getting up again. Dust blasts past with enough force it's like sandpaper. My ears pop. An entire door sails over both our heads. Suddenly, everything is coated white.

Peacock Dude looks up at the gaping doorway with his jaw hanging open. His surprised shout sounds like it's coming from several blocks away.

I buck, thrusting my hips upward. He's heavy, but I lift him an inch. Just enough. I shove against his knee and slide myself out from under him. He catches my belt-buckle but I've gone far enough. My fingers close on the Killer's grip.

"Die!" His shout pierces the muffling tone ringing in my ears.

The Killer flashes. A hole opens in his face and his other eyeball bursts. On the ceiling behind his head, a water blister explodes with a spray of hot vapor.

"Feeling's mutual," I tell him, as he falls off me. That colored hair curls in on itself, emitting an acrid, chemical steam.

Sagging paint blisters on the ceiling drip water that smells like a sewer. I wanna both hold my breath against the stink and breath all the air left in the world. I settle for laying still a few seconds and counting the drops against my face. Vapor from the Killer's shot makes the air like a steam sauna.

"Jin?" I shout. "Jin? Are you okay?"

"We're here." Her answer comes from the beyond bombed out doorway, in the tone of a cat who's gotten lost in a closet.

I have Peacock Guy's corpse steam on my skin. My stomach rolls but Max has to be harder than that. Max the Killer must know her trade.

I sit up, rest The Killer next to me, and lift my right wrist into my lap. Then I run my good hand over the knife wound. It's bleeding in earnest now but not the spurting pulse of an artery. So, not as bad as it could be. Still, that maw beneath me is pulling pretty hard, and it's getting tougher to tread water as I lose shoulders and hands.

"Jin are you okay?" I call again, but she doesn't reply.

My jacket makes a decent sling with the sleeve tied to the waist. If only this were the first time I've had to do that. It's why I wear a jacket with too-long sleeves folded up. Stopwatch says the Police should be here in seven minutes or less.

I stand and lift The Killer in my one hand. Three shots in the tank. The charger must have gotten its job done before it was knocked loose.

"Jin?" I call again, as I make my way through the empty doorframe. Some of the ceiling has come down in places, but only where the water's worn it through – the rest of the concrete still stands. White dust hangs in the air, flowing sluggishly in a breeze that comes in the broken door and moves out the shattered windows.

A pile of fallen junk holds the bedroom door open. Coin-sized holes speckle the living-room walls. A bunch of brick shards slither off one wall and across the floor.

Streaks of white dust like rays of a cartoon sun point at the epicenter of the blast: the column between the two windows. Right where the sink-5 used to be.

In the center of the biggest of those rays of dust crouches Jin. Her rope hangs in at the open window, connecting to her belt. Her black leathers shine clean, undusted, and she's left no footprints in the white-covered floor. It's like she swung in the blasted out window and alighted just exactly where she is now – making a black period in the white room. She crouches over the safe in the floor where I put my papers. It's open. Her hands are full.

"It was not a sink-5," she says, without looking up.

"No?" I wheeze, leaning against the bedroom wall, which sags a little.

"No. Sink-9. External explosive."

"I could never tell the difference."

"The 9 is much harder to disarm, but a smaller bomb."

"You just let it go off?" I can't mask my annoyance. "Lucky I wasn't waiting by the door."

"Yes. Lucky."

She's shifting through passports. She studies the cover of one for a moment before tossing it at my feet. It leaves a little scar in the dust. The cover says Republic of

Algiers. I don't need to open it to know she's found the real one. On the back page will be my letters of commission to the Inquisition.

Jin watches my face. She didn't open it. She pulled it out of a stack of fakes without opening it.

She knew.

The breeze moves its river of dust out the windows. I'm caught in the undertow.

A bit more junk falls out of the ceiling and patters onto the floor.

"So," I say, as my stomach curls up in my toes. "How long?"

Her eyes shine: "Work went bad when you were around. Hunters always close behind. Never enough so it was clear. We dug after Hong-Kong. Lots of us thought maybe. No-one was sure. You were good."

"Thanks." The Killer's heavy in my left hand. Like a diving weight. "You know they burned me right? That was Hong-Kong. I'm on the wind now."

"Yeah," she says, but doesn't blink.

She raises her right hand above her head, and then closes it into a fist. It looks like a signal.

Of course it's a signal. The only way the bad could get deeper is if Set's been lining up a rifle from the building across the street, and Jin came in here only and for no other reason than to double-check my guilt before she signed for the kill.

So I dive for cover.

The bullet zips in through the broken window to blast a hole in the wall above me a moment before the shot makes echoes outside. I'm already rolling into the bedroom.

"Set been lining up on me this whole time?" I shout. "That any way to treat a friend?"

"Eat yourself." Her words are whispered, but I hear them loud and clear.

A second rifle-shot tears through the interior wall like cobweb and punches on through the opposite side of the room. I rise to a crouch and get ready to run for it.

Jin springs off the hall wall and comes through the bedroom door at head height. Her left hand makes a claw and it scythes through the air just above my head as I duck. She lands a full pace behind me. I sprint into the hall, firing wildly toward the window as I go. The flash makes all the hanging dust shine in a wall of light. Another sniper-shot tears past me, rustling the cloth on my right shoulder.

Then I'm in the hallway and leaping over Peacock Guy's corpse. I round the corner by the elevators and press my back to the wall. No windows here. Set can't shoot me. Slight improvement, but the water's still deep and I don't see any lifeboats lining up. I could run, but all Jin has to do is put the word out and both sides of the law will want my corpse for exhibition.

"Jin? We need to talk!" I glance back around the corner. The hall's empty except for the body, fallen door, and dust.

Water trickles down my neck from the leak in the ceiling. Chalky dust cloys to my sweat. I must look a fright. I wonder when that got to be normal?

"Remember O'Conner?" Her voice echoes from every which way. "Caught a bullet in the brain in Berlin?"

"Yeah that sucked. I liked O'Conner. He was funny. You know where he got his teeth though? He cannibalized one of Cardinal Montmore's hunting-dogs. Montmore caught up. That's what happens."

I risk a sprint past the elevator to punch its summons button, but I don't stop in the open next to the gaping gate. Instead, I head down the hall a few doors and shoulder one open. Another empty, cookie-cutter apartment.

The lights all go out at once. Neat trick. I reach for my goggles with my right hand before pain reminds me the hand's broken. I have to crouch and set my gun down to get the goggles in place.

"Have you seen Thunder since prison?" Jin's voice comes from the hall.

"I didn't know they'd let her out." It's good she's talking. We need to keep talking.

"They put a bug in her brain. One of those little hooks. Now she's a citizen. Married. Two soft children."

"Thunder? You're kidding." I lean out the door-jam and scan the hall. The Killer's light fills it. Nothing moves but the pathetic bumping of the elevator gate trying to close.

"She votes." Jin makes that a condemnation most vile.

I whip around. She spoke too soon – still a dozen paces down the hall, but moving fast. Her right hand tears the bulging wall-paper and water springs out of it, making my goggle display shimmer with golden snow. Through the haze of it, my shot goes wide. Then she springs – a two meter high pounce that lets her clawed fingers tear a gash in the water-logged ceiling. Water pours out, making a torrent of shimmering golden snow in which that leap carries her toward me like a swooping crow. I could make the shot. Even with the dust, even with the glitter everywhere. I could make the shot. But then Jin would be dead.

So I don't.

Her right hand loops and twists the Killer from my fingers. Her left fist plants bone-knuckles against my chin. I roll with the blow, though it cuts my lips against my teeth, and come back with a left hook that she blocks with her elbow. She steps back and tosses my weapon behind her. The light from its barrel turns her into a black silhouette and plays off the waterfall, filling the hall with glimmering reflections.

"Grendal Jackson," she snarls, as I back away with my guard up. "Cut-man who fixed these eyes? Coppers put him in a metal chair."

She's shorter than me, and her left jab and right straight angle up at my face. I duck the jab and block the straight.

"Jin, please-" before I can finish the phrase she's slapped the side of my head and made my goggles flicker and the image sway.

"You know why? He affixed limbs. When he couldn't sell one he'd give it to an orphan. A hobby."

While my goggles adjust, her fists pile into my stomach and cheeks. I keep backing away, twisting and turning. I taught her to fight. I'm better than her. I should be, but she's caught my jacket and spun me to my left. My foot goes off a gap. I fall backward, but she holds me up, and then my foot found an edge.

It's raining on my head. A wind rushes up at me from behind. My vision clears.

I hang by my jacket front, leaning back into the elevator shaft. Rusty water patters down around me. The elevator's coming down toward us, somewhere above, just a glinting bit of metal approaching through the shadows.

She studies me down the length of her arms. Her deep stance plants her legs wide as she supports my weight. My arms hang tired, my fingers barely able to grip her wrist. I can't tell if she says the words out loud, or if I see them in those mismatched eyes all cracked and broken:

I loved you.

"Jin," I try, but split lips, thin breath and a spinning world stop me.

"I came here to burry my past." I try again. "I was on the wrong side."

"Poppy-smoke," she whispers. "They turned on you. Now you turn on them."

"Please," I beg. My heart is a winged bird caught in a too tight fist. "You've got to admit we were always good together. Let me help you. You're all I have left. I've got no other choice."

"No," she says. "You don't. But I do."

And she lets go.

Rust-flavored rain falls around me. Wind kisses the back of my neck.

That fluttering heart tries to climb out of my chest through the knife-wound. It splashes tears into my eyes.

I hit bottom like a bell.

Disciples

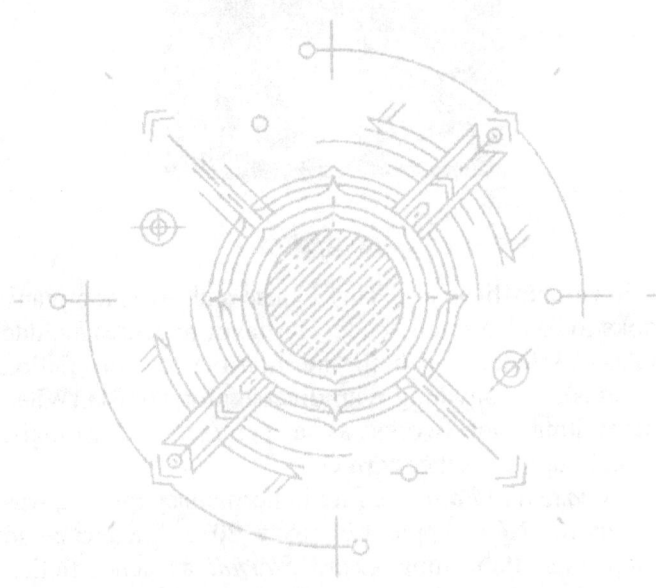

V. S. HOLMES

V. S. HOLMES

Disciples

V. S. Holmes lives in a Tiny House and owns too many books for such a small abode. Her favorite genres include fantasy, science (of both the non-fiction and fiction varieties), and anything with diverse protagonists. When not writing, she works as a contract archaeologist throughout the northeastern U.S.

Smoke and Rain, the first in her fantasy quartet, was chosen for New Apple Literary's 2015 Excellence in Independent Publishing Award. *Starfall*, a science-fiction short can be found in the January 2016 issue of *Vitality*, an LGBT magazine.

She can be found at her website as well as on Facebook, Twitter, Goodreads, and Instagram.

www.vs-holmes.com

Disciples

V. S. HOLMES

CHAPTER ONE

Cryosleep was a temporary death. The lights were dim, a twilight between waking and sleep. Lin blinked and rolled her shoulders, stretched her neck, curled her toes. Viscous stasis fluid drained silently, leaving goosebumps across her beige skin. Nausea shuddered through her. She ignored it. Instead she drifted in the peace of momentary amnesia. The hiss of heated air punctured the stillness. She flexed her fingers and tapped the smooth metal embedded in the flesh of her wrist. "Commence waking sequence in five…." She counted the seconds down silently.

"Good morning, Opsir Nalawangsa." The low voice was male, and just shy of truly human. The lights rose, gradual and faintly yellow.

"Good morning, Phil. Where are we?" She pushed out of her tank, rising in the zero G of her cryo tube. The lights were fully bright now.

"We're in orbit, 437 km from the surface of the planet Earth." There was a pause, and she almost thought the ship's voice held a smile. "Welcome home."

She snorted. "My genes may come from that ball of dirt, Phil, but I certainly don't." The air rolled over her skin, drying as it went. A click and pop echoed from beside the closed door of the cryo tube. She grabbed the vial from the ship's delivery system and held it up.

NALAWANGSA, LIN
IMMUNIZATION LEVEL 2
STABILIZERS
PROTEIN
CARBOHYDRATES
ELECTROLYTES
VITAMINS A, D, B, C
SALINE

She groaned. "What does a woman have to do to get proper grilled fish with her breakfast in bed?"

"When you cure cryo-sick I will personally deliver you a plate of fresh milkfish in bed upon waking."

She rolled her eyes and snapped the vial into the port in her arm. A moment passed then her nausea subsided. Aching in her head ebbed. "How was the trip?"

"Uneventful. You are wanted in Trajectory." Phil's tone often trod the line between a butler's deference and a captain's rebuke.

"Dar?"

"Yes. It appears Komodor Muda Nalawangsa has requested you personally. Shall I tell him you're on your way?" *Probably just to rub in his new rank of Komodor Muda and the fact he's now senior enough to just 'request' me.* "Thanks, Phil. I'll see you there." She unwrapped the plastic from her uniform and slid it on. After seven years of drifting naked in a vat of saline, the stiff electro-fiber felt cumbersome. She flexed her hand, aligning the contacts inside with the conduits tattooed on her skin. A hum. A rush of energy not-quite-her-own. *Paired.* The word wasn't spoken, not heard in the traditional sense, nor was it a thought. It least, not hers. *Increase temperature by 0.5 degrees C.*

Her goosebumps sank back into her skin. She slid the door open and slithered from her cryotube. The lights here were brighter, the snaking lines of green and blue illuminating the stark white of walls and the sharp sliver of glass. Her finger brushed the pad in the wall, changing a panel from cycling photos to a mirror. She scraped her hair back and straightened her collar. It was always alarming how little her face changed during years of cryosleep. She wondered when she could return to her work curating their ancestors' history.

"Opsir Nalawangsa—"

"Yeah, Phil, I know. On my way." She shoved through the next door into a corridor. The steep curve told her still-disoriented mind she was on the interior of the ship. A gentle press indicated they were just inside the gravitational field. *Planet-side is starboard.* She kicked off the floor and sailed along the corridor. Other than several bots and the usual techs, the hall was deserted. *Debriefing already started then.* It took days for the ship and crew to recover from a cryo-trip to open space. Longer when they arrived at a planet's orbit. She found the first drop-door to the exterior rings of the ship and pressed the symbol for Trajectory. The ground trembled with the rings' gentle turning. When the doors between the outer rings and a transport shaft were aligned the door slid open. Lin dropped, her grin broad. This was her favorite part. The slight artificial gravity brought by the rotation grew the farther from the core she got, so what started as a gentle drift accelerated into a true free fall.

WARNING: Falling from high places can result in damage or expiration. Engage mag-catch. She ignored the suit for another moment, enjoying the rushing air. Lights flickered past as she hurtled through dozens of levels. She clenched her teeth against biting her tongue. *Suit: Engage mag-catch.* Electromagnets in her suit kicked on with a hum and lurch. By the time she arrived at the door emblazoned with the symbol for Trajectory she was floating. A panel slid across the transport tube and she touched down. Gravity settled over her like a blanket. Even her organs felt heavy. Her palm on the door granted access to the waiting area. Another palm on the next door prompted a cheery robotic voice very unlike Phil's.

"Good morning! Please state your rank, full name, and purpose clearly into the speaker."

Lin leaned forward. "Opsir Muda Udara First Class Lin Nalawangsa, to see Komodor Muda Udara Dar Nalawangsa."

"Accepted, have a lovely day!"

Lin smiled, wondering if the security bot's voice grew irate when you weren't allowed through. The door slid open and she stepped through. Trajectory was as messy and chaotic as the rest of the ship was tidy. The bank of screens to the left showed their past trips, and those of other ships in the fleet. One blinked with a digital scan of Phil's face as he debriefed the crew and discussed issues with other ships' minds. The right was a whirlwind of orbit physics and gravitational maps. Her brother stood within the ring of navigation and communication computers that dominated the center of the room. He snarled something at the image of Phil's head on one of his screens. "I don't really care what the ISS has to say. Our orbit takes precedence. It's much harder for us to navigate then for them."

"Sir," Phil offered, "I think they feel differently. They're expecting a shipment and new crew. Their flightpath has been planned for months, and the weather won't hold forever—"

"I'll show them fucking weather..." His mutter almost drowned in a chorus of beeps that rose from Navigation. "Then put me on the com with NASA."

"Paging NASA."

Lin saw her opening and stepped up to the raised floor of the Captain's Ring. "You wanted to see me, Dar?"

Dar frowned, but did not look up. He could have been her twin: black, smooth hair, warm beige skin, and deep oval eyes. Their features and parents, however, were the only things they shared.

"I need you to go planet-side."

Lin's stomach lurched. The tingle crawling up her arms had nothing to do with electromagnets or her suit maintaining temperature. "Excuse me?"

"You heard me, Lin, I don't have time to play coy. You're going planet-side. Loading should begin in 14 hrs, assuming NASA gets their heads out of their arses."

"I've never been planet-side."

"You've been five times."

"As a child, Dar, this is different." *What mission do we possibly have on Earth?* It had been decades since anyone bothered to interfere from above. Their Institute ran things well from their Headquarters on the planet itself. Touching down meant something changed. And the Institute always prepared for everything. *So it's an emergency if they're calling us in.* "What happened?"

"Someone is about to discover where we started. Where the Amba first found us."

"Isn't that what we want? What the Institute wants?"

"Yes, of course. Earth can't develop without understanding our role, but this is sooner than we wanted, sooner than we planned. Clearly someone at the Institute itself helped permits along, and believe me, there will be an investigation into who that person is, but for now, the most we can do is monitor the situation. And monitoring the situation is best done in the field, as it were."

Lin wished there was a chair to sit in, a moment of peace from the shrill beeps and insistent chimes so she could sink her head in her hands to think. *I don't want to go planet-side. I don't know anyone there. I have work here.* In space, the Institute was everywhere, a personal, constant parental figure like the Amba had been—all the more loving due to their mother being in charge of the entire Exploration Department. On earth, the Institute was a distant, classified branch of every countries' government. Even if they didn't realize it. "14 hours? What about my work?"

"You can return to it once this is through. This mission takes priority. You'll be briefed on the situation shortly, but for now you ought to pack your necessities."

"Why aren't they sending you? I thought this was what you dreamed of?"

Dar shot her a glare, whether for the dare of questioning orders, or the embarrassment of her bringing up his personal aspirations in public, she wasn't sure. "My greatest wish is to see the rest of our people raised to our level of technology. The stars are the final exploratory frontier, Lin. They won't get there without us. You know that. I have more pressing matters to handle here. You had the same education I did, so you'll have to do in my stead."

Lin's heart was accustomed to his condescension. It still stung. "Of course. I'll stand-by for briefing, then."

"Oh, I almost forgot." Dar tilted his head, as if Phil could somehow hear him better. "Philos, Update Rank: Lin Nalawangsa."

Lin glanced down at the tingle of electricity passing through the fibers of her suit. The bands across her chest and around each limb flickered then changed to red.

Anger filled her body, following the echo of electricity. "I'm demoted?"

"You're reassigned."

"Opsir Muda Udara First Class to Letnan First Class is a demotion," she reiterated.

"It's a lateral move and certainly not up for discussion. That is all." He turned away, as if she ceased to exist at his dismissal.

She bit back her response and left the room before anyone saw her angry tears. The door to the transport tube slid open, shut. For a moment she was cocooned in the visual static of flickering lights and silence. *Letnan First Class Lin Nalawangsa.* A terrestrial rank, rather than aeronautical. It tasted bitter in her mouth.

CHAPTER TWO

"I thought the site was in the mountains where no one would find it. Unless they were looking for it." Lin peered down at the faint blue glow of her mission details. It was a sea of maps and personnel files. The Institute had made sure development was bureaucratically impossible. "And from what Dar said, no one was supposed to be looking for it."

"You're familiar with archaeology?" Several people crowded around the table. All except she and Dar bore the luminescent white of the Institute's science division marking their suits. The woman who spoke had a doctorate's badge on her shoulder displaying the name "Ndebele."

"The excavation and study of past human settlement, culture, and evolution." If there was one thing Lin was good at, it was the recall of information.

"Someone applied for archaeological permits for the area. And miraculously they were granted." The woman clarified.

They will be dealt with and terminated. Lin wondered how permanently "terminated" it would be. *Terminated from their career or from life?* "So someone at the Institute is a Founder. No, that doesn't make sense, the Founders want everything about us and where we came from to remain hidden from the public."

"As far as we know, yes, that's still the case. This person was probably a radical, someone with more hope in humanity than we currently have. God willing we will be able to mitigate the damage this might cause," Ndebele murmured.

Lin looked at the personnel files. As much as she shared the genetic makeup with the eight billion people floating on the rock beneath her, she could not have felt more different. *Alien.* But she would never have said they were beyond hope. Perhaps it was because her parents protected her from human horrors whenever they touched down as children. Perhaps she just was still young enough to know the warmth of hope. "What am I supposed to do, sabotage the site?"

"I'm sure they'll face enough of that from the Founders. There's a strong presence there, on account of the location. I want you to monitor. Report. If they need help, we'll handle it."

"Couldn't I help?"

"Just because this is a little ahead of schedule doesn't mean we don't want it meticulous, Lin. You have some experience, but a full team would be beneficial if contact is made."

"Moreover, the more the team discovers on their own, the easier the news will be to process for the Terrestrial humans. Help should only be needed if something goes incredibly wrong." The deep voice rumbled from the speaker in the center of the table and she looked up to the previously blank holoscreen.

"Ayah?"

Her father's face softened slightly, but he did not humor her casual greeting with a response. "We will handle this just as we always have—control and objectivity."

"Sir, begging your pardon, but don't you feel we would be better off cutting the funding and forcing the old man who wants to dig it up to wait?" Dar asked.

Lin tapped one of the personnel files. The picture was grainy, but the stats below it were clear. "Woman."

"Excuse me?" Dar turned the force of his gaze on her.

She bit her lip, wondering if their father heard the disdain. "The doctor heading the dig—it's a young woman."

"At any rate," their father interjected, "I have decided we will, indeed, help this excavation. It is not up for discussion, Dar." His brown eyes flicked to Lin. "Lin, these files will be downloaded to your suit and your personal device. I suggest you look them over while you are still on board. Touch-down is in—"

"T-4.15 hours. I know."

A young man with a low-level sci-tech symbol on his shoulder leaned forward with a frown. "Don't you feel it is dangerous to involve ourselves so directly?"

Ndebele shook her head. "I'm sure Lin will find a way to make the Institute's reach less...apparent. Dr. Bently knows we are the group that funded her grant. Surely that's all she needs to know."

Lin forced her hands into stillness in her lap. *Make sure they find what they need to. Make sure they're safe. Do the job, get off the planet.* It would be her mantra for the next few weeks.

"If there are no further questions?" Her father's voice paused, then when no one spoke, he ordered, "Dismissed."

She did not move from her seat. The others filed out, conversation rising like a muttered tide as they returned to other, less pressing tasks. Her father remained on the screen, his gentle eyes fixed on hers. "Ayah, could I have a word?"

"I've got a meeting in five minutes. I'm yours until then." He leaned forward.

Lin could almost smell the scent of soil and pine. They were on Earth the last time she saw him—truly saw him, in person, not through the pixels of digital conversation. *37 years ago. 17 cercadial years.* They had visited a forest, almost as large as the one powering the space station where she had been born.

"What's wrong, Dewdrop?"

She smiled at the pet name. "My stomach keeps twisting in knots. I know this is what we want—them to find us, learn from us—but this feels fast. And wrong. Ibu always says to trust my instincts."

"And you should. But sometimes we are so wrapped up in what we think the problem will be, we don't see what your brain is actually warning us about."

"And what do you think my brain is warning me about?" She searched his face for an answer.

"I don't know, but I think you need to have some trust."

"In Dar?" She couldn't hide the skepticism from her words. Their parents loved them both, but they knew Dar and Lin would never be the best friends some siblings were.

"Not necessarily, no. You are worried about the terrestrials being cruel, not being ready. You're worried that this will go wrong and destroy your reputation, and Dar's as well?"

"A bit, I think." *I'm more worried about what Dar will do with me when I mess everything up. I can see it now. Demoted to working a back-water ship lightyears from everyone I know.*

"Well let me explain something to you." An insistent beeping began on his end. He waved a hand and it silenced.

Before he continued Lin shook her head. "You're going to be late to your meeting. Tell me later, when I've touched down."

"You sure?"

She smiled, pulling happiness she did not feel on to her face. "Sure. I'll be alright."

He seemed unconvinced, but nodded. "Send me a message when you're settled in down there. You'll do fine, Lin." He shot her a broad smile and the screen went black.

Lin drew a deep breath, then another. *Trust.*

"Letnan Nalawangsa, you're expected in Medical for your scans and immunizations in 15 minutes."

"Thanks, Phil. I'll be right down."

She pushed off down the corridor to the passenger bunks. She hadn't even had the chance to sleep in hers. Though her things were all where she had stowed them, it felt like someone else's room. Her personal device, an extra suit. Nothing else seemed necessary. Earth was a different world, and whatever she thought to bring with her would only raise more questions. The downside to never bringing personal items was nothing ever felt like home.

She shook off the surge of melancholy. Coming out of cryo was always an adjustment. Too many feelings and too little connection. She used the transport tube properly this time, her brother's castigation still loud in her ears. Medical was deeper into the interior of the ship, the expensive, sensitive equipment protected from debris by hundreds of layers of steel. The halls were crowded, and she was ushered to the end of the row of individual bays. *I wonder how many others are going with me? Will I have a team?* It hadn't sounded like she would have much company, but then again, she imagined there were other missions.

A medical doctor stepped in and flashed Lin a smile. She was tall, her halo of thick black curls held back with a surgical hat. "Morning, Letnan. I'll just need your arm bare today. How are you doing? Adjusting to post-cryo alright?"

"A little moody. Mostly fine." Lin stripped the left arm of her suit off, grateful that was all. The padded table was warm, but not enough to be comfortable. The doctor checked her vitals, her range of motion. A slim metal device plugged into her port tested her blood levels.

"You seem to be adjusting just fine."

Lin eyed the row of vials on the tray beside her. "All that? This isn't my first trip."

"There are some really bad strains down there. You'd think with the help we give their doctors they'd have figured out the solution by now." The doctor shrugged, pursing her broad lips. "Too wrapped up in the money to pay attention."

The third vial clicked into Lin's port and she winced at the tingle. She was used to this, but somehow the sensation never grew familiar. She pointed to the fourth. It was a thick substance, the translucent liquid tinged blue. "What's that one?"

"Mild anesthetic and neurodampener. Just to be safe for the upgrade."

"Upgrade?"

"You're receiving an update to your conduit." The doctor tapped a brown finger on Lin's tattoo. The black line wound from the nape of her neck, down the side of her throat and to the circle where it connected to her suit. "They didn't tell you?"

Lin frowned. "Why? The suit paired just fine this morning."

"It's not for your suit, Letnan. It's for your glove." The doctor popped the blue vial into the port.

Lin's brows shot up. The only thing that kept her still was the sudden heaviness in her limbs. "I don't use gloves. I'm not a soldier. Gloves are weapons."

The doctor fixed her with a puzzled stare. "I was told you were touching down. Did I misunderstand?"

"No, Doctor, but I don't see what that has to do with anything."

"When was the last time you were on Earth?"

"32 earth-years ago. 17 circadial time. Why?" A heavy darkness loomed in her gut. It was the same feeling she got when Phil sounded sad, or when her parents were late arriving out of lightspeed. *Dread.* Her suit buzzed, counter-acting the sudden chill the spread over her skin. It tightened, compressing her limbs in a way she supposed was intended to be comforting. "Why?" She asked again.

"Letnan, the Earth has changed a lot. You're not just monitoring the excavation and discovery of the site. You're protecting it, and our various assets—human and otherwise—from damage. The Founders have a heavy presence in the area. And their reach is growing further each day. As is their determination."

"Their violence, you mean. I thought we weren't a military."

"The institute has many departments. And you've just been transferred to our Military." The doctor seemed to catch the shock on her face, and softened her voice. "I was told you were informed about all of this."

"They phrased this as a preservation mission."

"It is, in a way." The doctor raised the slim, white tattoo machine and conduit feed. "Preservation of life. You'll need a weapon to do your job. May I?"

Lin nodded, her head falling back on the chair's headrest. The injection of the conduit wasn't painless, but itched more than it stung. The burn trailed down her arm in the wake of the machine, black line following the line of humerus, radius, carpals, terminating in a fork at the proximal phalanges of her index and thumb. The thin line would transmit a signal from her mind to a weapon. A thin line enabling her to kill as easily as she changed her suit's temperature.

The outfitting was quick, as quick as her packing had been: an extra suit, enough communication power to contact to the ship even from the desert. Now, in the solitude of her room, she ran a hand over the electrofiber glove. "I don't really know how to use this," she confessed to the room.

"You won't need to use it until you're in the field, and even then, we'd prefer diplomacy." Her brother appeared in the doorway. His voice was low.

"I've been trained, but it was years ago, and non-integrated." Lin flexed her hand and finally turned to look at Dar. He stood in the doorway, looking somehow smaller without his official collar. She could pick out the similarities between their tall, thin bodies, despite them hopscotching in age and years from the stasis of travel. *Ibu's hands. Ayah's shoulders. Both's height. Neither's stance.* "I've to go soon."

"I know the departure time. I thought I ought to say goodbye."

"You'll pick me up when I'm done?"

"Assuming it doesn't take years, yes. Once the discovery is made and published, a team from the PR department will take over for you. You don't have to deal with that, at least. I know you're not too fond of the humans down there."

"I don't mind them, I just don't understand them. All so desperate, burning their lives up so fast."

"We're the same, you know."

She lifted her shoulder in a shrug and sank onto the couch. "I don't see it. Genetically, sure, but otherwise? We study the difference between closely related species, and its really just if they can breed. Sometimes it's just the behaviors are so different the two groups can't."

"Lin, we're not different species. You can't even argue we're difference 'races' as they would put it."

"That's just it, Dar, they still believe in things like race and God—"

"Plenty of our people believe in higher powers too. Our trust in the Amba borders on faith."

"It just feels different."

His gaze slid past her and to the distant curve peeking above the edge of her window. "We're from there." He repeated. His expression was more than curiosity now. Unveiled before her, it was reverent, as if he looked on something sacred. She realized, perhaps to him, it was.

"We're from *Odyssey*."

"You know what I mean. Not originally. Don't you want to know what our ancestors were like?"

"We have stories, documents from the Amba, we've curated species they drove extinct down there."

His smile was brief. "I doubt that's everything." He straightened and offered his hands. "I'll be seeing you off from Trajectory."

She pushed herself to her feet and hugged him. As much as he was mercurial, he was her brother first. "I'll talk to you when I'm settled. And I'll let you know how things look on the ground once I get a better idea."

"Lin," he rumbled against her shoulder. "You be careful. It's not the same Earth as when you were little."

"I'm not the same either." It was a lie, she felt. She was just as ill prepared and young—if not literally— than when she stepped off the transport as a child. "I'll be fine."

He pulled away, clapped her shoulder like she was his air-light buddy, and disappeared into the hall.

"REPORT TO LOADING BAY TANGO: DOCTOR NDEBELE, KELASI JACKSON, PRADJURIT FIRST CLASS SHAH, LETNAN FIRST CLASS NALAWANGSA, LETNAN LAUT LOPEZ. DEPARTURE IN T-28.3 MINUTES."

Nerves exploded in Lin's gut. It took all her might, all the echoes of her father's words to wrench her feet from the floor and close her case. *I'll be fine.* The corridors were crowded now, at least one stage of debriefing over with. The loading bays dotted the external edge of the outermost ring, but she could not bring herself to freefall now. The red on her suit burned in her mind and she hoped her embarrassment did not show on her cheeks.

The doors to the bay were open, the great outer doors still sealed tightly against the void of space. She tugged on the additional layer to her suit and plugged the wires into her port and the tiny hole at her clavicle that served as additional conduit attachment. The helm sealed out the sounds, the hissing the rumble, the chatter. For a perfect moment, she refused to turn the coms on. Two ships crouched in the bay, one smaller craft for half a dozen people, and the typical larger shuttle for hundreds. She wondered what excuse NASA would give the public, those who still bothered to tear their gaze from their navels long enough to look up at the stars.

She moved up the gangway for the larger craft. Sharp knocking rattled her helmet. She turned. The young man behind her pointed at his ear and mouthed, exaggerated, "Your com not working?" His hair was slicked back at the top from running his engine-greased hand through it, but curly tufts spiraled out from his ears like angry steam.

She winced and flicked it on. "Sorry it's been a long day."

"You're on the wrong ship. You're riding the *Thunder-Bump* down with me, not this one. I'm Bavin."

She eyed the smaller ship, the hull dinged and scratched from a dozen entries. She had only ever flown in the larger shuttles. Who named their ship *Thunder-bump* anyway? "Where's the shuttle going?"

"To Headquarters, as usual."

"And this one?"

"We're headed to ALMA." He beckoned her back down the gangway and under the belly of the crouched *Thunder-bump*. "This way."

"Where's that?"

He rolled his eyes. "Long day indeed. Not where, what."

"What is it then?"

"ALMA. Atacama Large Millimeter/submillimeter Array. One of our bigger telescope arrays. Also one of the better hidden airstrips we have. Plus it's closer to the site by several thousand miles." He grinned. "And it's a much more exciting entry."

Lin groaned. "I haven't touched down here in years. I'm not sure exciting is my thing."

"You'll come around." Bavin threw her case into the yawning maw of the cargo bay, following it with a few packages and a box of what looked like a variety pack of suits. After a second he paused and fixed Lin with a meaningful eye. "You wanna help, here?" He indicated the pile of heaped boxes and cases waiting to be loaded. "*Thunder-bump* ain't gonna load herself."

Lin shrugged and set to work. They were tossing in the last few cases when the alarm blared. She flinched and looked up.

"BAY DOORS OPENING IN T-1.4 MINUTES. IF YOU ARE NOT TOUCHING DOWN TODAY OR A BAY-HAND PLEASE RETURN TO THE *PROMISE*. ALL CREW AND PASSENGERS SHOULD WEAR HELMETS AT THIS TIME."

Lin double-checked the seal and lock on her space suit. Bavin still bounced around, hair like Saturn's rings around the mass of his skull.

"FLIGHT CHECK FOR 35T-872 *THUNDER-BUMP* BEGINNING."

"We're next, load up." He smacked the side of his craft and hauled himself hand-over-hand onto the wing before disappearing into the cockpit. When Lin didn't follow, his voice crackled in her ear. "Up here, missy, you're riding with me."

She drew a breath and followed him. She barely listened as he chattered into the coms to flight control. She checked her belt again, biting back a shriek when the craft dropped through the yawning bay doorway.

The craft rumbled, air screaming over the nose as they plunged deeper into the atmosphere. Her lungs burned at the effort to inflate against the thrust of gravity. *2Gs. 3Gs.* Thoughts slowed, time taking the scenic route through the winding neurons in her brain. Whooping filled the coms as fire exploded past the window.

"There go our heat shields, baby!"

She closed her eyes, as much due to impending unconsciousness as her companion's disregard for safety.

"Touching down in Antofagasta, Airstrip ALMA in 12...11...."

She glanced out the window, letting Bavin's countdown fade into the cacophony of beeping, trilling instruments. Below lay the red sea of sand. The airstrip was a white scar across it. Glittering on the horizon told her they were west of the array of telescopes. Lurching knocked her back into full consciousness.

"Terrestrial flight mode: Engage."

The back half of the craft blew away. The parachutes deployed. The landing gear ground out, somehow unharmed by the flames earlier.

He grinned, eyes as wild as the flight she just survived. "Welcome to Planet Earth, Letnan Nalawangsa."

CHAPTER THREE

The first thing she noticed was the air. Before, she could not have named the scent of home if she had to. *Nothing.* Home smelled of nothing. Sterile. Here, however, were hundreds of scents. Most with no name in her mind, just vague ideas, or colors. *There.* A hot, dry smell of sand. The warmth of brown vegetation desiccating in the sun. Sweat. *I haven't smelled sweat in years.*

"Dan will get you to the labs where you'll work." Bavin explained, handing down her bag.

She offered what she was sure was a wan smile. "Thanks, Bavin. I'll be sure to fly with you again." She stumbled, found her footing on the second try. "Though perhaps not soon."

He cackled and disappeared into the maw of the *Thunder-bump.*

She emerged from the hanger, eyes shielded against the piecing desert light. When she scraped a hand through her hair it caught in new tangles. She winced.

"Letnan Nalawangsa!"

A jeep idled by the hanger, the driver leaning on the battered rollcage. His white tank top and khakis were quite the change from the uniforms on her ship. She felt suddenly shy, as if she had overdressed but no one had the heart to point it out. She shouldered her bag and raised a hand.

When she was close enough not to shout over the wind she smiled. "You can call me Lin." Anything was better than hearing her new rank.

"Lin, then. I'm Dr. Danilo Sanlinas, I do a lot of the microscopy and chem analysis here. Mostly though," he held out his hand, dark eyes flashing, "I answer the phones."

She laughed, then frowned at the offered hand.

"Right, you guys don't shake hands, just do that palm-touch thing, like you're looking in a mirror. You never been Dirt-side?" His incredulity was kind, despite the raised brows.

"I have, but it was years ago." She extended a tentative hand, which he gripped firmly and shook. "I was a child."

"Que bueno. Hop in, we can go get you settled." He glanced over. "Your Spanish is good."

"It was my second language after Amalga." She tossed her bag into the back and clambered into the seat Dan indicated. "Hopefully the drive is easier than the flight down."

Dan chuckled. "Bavin is quite the pilot, but he forgets not everyone is as comfortable in the cockpit as he."

The road was indeed less bumpy than her flight, but only just. The sprawl of buildings that emerged from the sand ahead were state-of-the-art, or had been perhaps ten years ago. Now the concrete was sandblasted and sunbleached. The white dome of the observatory loomed over the rest of the complex, a great fossilized egg forgotten in the sands. "The Institute owns this?"

"Not the gleaming sci-fi mega-complex you expected, eh?"

"No, not really."

"Gotta blend in here. Most governments don't think space is a worthwhile place to sink money, and it'd be suspicious if we looked shiny and new. Plus, most of your funding goes to Headquarters and various other more…political projects.

Lin glanced over, wondering at the pause. It was no secret that the Institute had their long, debatably alien fingers in most of Earth's more influential cookie jars. She always thought it was out of benevolence. Dan's hesitation made her wonder. They drove down into a basement garage bay and rumbled to a halt. The sand drifted into stillness and Lin heaved a sigh. It always struck her how much more violent terrestrial travel was in comparison to space, despite being exponentially slower. Their lives, too, were the epitome of burning bright, burning fast, burning out. It was something she feared she would never understand.

"We do rotations out here, but I'll be here for the next three months. How long you down for?" He tugged her bag from the back seat and handed it to her.

"No longer than three months, I hope." It was a sickening thought, being stuck down here with no one she knew, doing surveillance.

Dan's laugh was a rasping bark, multiplied by the hard metal of the long hallway he led her down. "Not a fan, eh?"

"Not really, no. I had other projects I wanted to take care of." *No I didn't.* She was curating an exhibit on the first encounters between their ancestors and the Amba when Dar received orders to enter cryo and fly to Earth. The data had waited 13,000 years. She knew nothing would change if it had to wait a few more. It was busy work, something for the less driven Nalawangsa child to occupy herself with while her brother saved the stars. Or whatever it was that Dar thought he did.

"Lin?"

"Hmm?"

"I was just explaining the layout of the buildings. You alright? You look a thousand miles away."

"I woke up from cryo less than 24 hrs ago. I'm a bit disoriented." It wasn't strictly true, but she didn't mind lying. "I'm sorry, please go on."

"Our dorms are on the north side of the back building. Labs are on the south. The main entrance and observatory are all on the other side of the compound." He gestured to various halls, each marked with a sign and arrows. Lin frowned. It would be an adjustment to actually read the words, rather than just follow the pictograms that the ships used for accessibility.

"Here we are." Dan waved his badge over a black pad by a heavy double door and typed in a few digits. "You'll get your badge tomorrow. We didn't know you were coming until a few hours ago. I guess there was an argument with NASA?"

"My brother doesn't take kindly to being told to wait."

"He in Trajectory?"

"He's the Komodor."

Dan grinned and held the door open for her. "That must be nice, get you out of trouble, does he?"

More like into it. "Sometimes." She followed him down the long, dingy hall. The low lights dragged at her energy. "These the dorms?"

"Us residents are on the left—we have suites since we live here—and you'll be on the right. You have a bathroom, shower, all that, but the kitchen is shared at the end of the hall."

Shower? It wasn't something they often used on ships. Conserving water was important and the suits took care of most hygiene aspects.

"There's some standard issue shirts and pants in there, and the city's not far if you need to grab anything else. We have a small commissary too, but that's just for sundries." He hung on the doorframe for a moment. "Go ahead and make yourself at home. I should get back to the microscope soon." He paused, seemingly not sure if she was listening. "Any questions?"

She dropped her bag on the low bed. *Home.* It was an alien concept, at least as far as a place was concerned. Her extra set of clothes went in the drawer of the wardrobe. Civilian clothes would come later. Now, despite the sun rising, all she wanted to do was sleep. "How long until Dr. Bently and her crew arrive?"

"She's landing in an hour. Picking up a rental and driving down to the site from there. They're staying in the town just south of the site. You want to receive her at the airport?"

She glanced up, sharply. *Meet Bently? Is that what I'm supposed to do?* "Meet her? I think I'll let them get settled in before I make ourselves known. It's best if they do what they can on their own, before too much meddling." *Plus, then I can figure out exactly what I'm supposed to do with myself.* She tapped her computer awake and opened the control page for her mission. It was straight-forward enough. The one thing she didn't have a handle on was the Founders.

If they had a strong presence, as her father worded it, then they would be easy to track. They didn't have the organization to erase their tracks, at least not well. She looked longingly at the bed. It had been hours since she woke up for the first time in years, but her body was exhausted. *No time.* She sighed. "I could use whatever stimulants you have available and I'd like to see my work station."

"Sure thing." He lead her down a series of hallways to a broad bank of windows. They looked into a Level 1 Lab, complete with computers—though these seemed to mostly be the simple Terrestrial versions. Dan held the door open for her. "You'll be over here, kitty-corner to where I am most of the time. This is sort of the monitoring area. You've got these three computers—lucky, you get two of our five good ones." He grinned at her. "Stim-u is here—" he pointed out the rack of vials. "If you're more into ingesting your caffeine, like I am, then you can do so in our employee lounge or the mess, or your room. No food or drinks in here though, sorry."

"I'll take this for now." She double checked the label on a red vial and clipped it into her radial port. She sank into the chair and tapped the screen of the first computer. Nothing happened. When she tried again, Dan laughed.

"We're not that advanced, Lin. You gotta use the mouse."

"Mouse?" She eyed the cage of the white lab mice through the glass in the next lab.

His laughter doubled. "No, no, the pointing device." He palmed the plastic blob on the pad next to the keypad. "Like this."

"It's a wonder they made it past the stone age."

"You're telling me." He handed her a list of passcodes and login information. "You all set?"

"I think for now. I'll ask if something comes up."

"Alright, I'm going to grab dinner. Want anything."

Lin hummed in negation, mind already set on the task ahead. She logged into the computers and accessed her Mission page through the employee portal. She needed to see and hear what Bently, her crew, and the Founders were doing, and fast. Until she had more information, she was hobbled.

After several minutes of struggling with the archaeic machines, she retrieved her device from her room. "Computer, can you pair with IP: 43.197.284.102 through the ALMA network?"

"That IP is not connected to the global net."

"Computer: Use your Terriestrial networking software."

"Accessing Terrestrial software. Pairing. Connected."

Lin smiled and set the device on her desk. It was so much easier to dictate then navigate the keypad, despite its convenient Dvorak layout. "Alright. Let's get down to business." It took a matter of minutes to access the video feed from various security cameras at the local restaurants, airport, and police station. The motel didn't seem to have one, but the house across the street had a private closed circuit showing the motel's front door and part of the driveway.

"Computer: scan of all communication to and from IP: 43.197.284.102 starting now. Alert words include:

abnormal, funding, Founders, Los Pobladores, vandalism, Institute...." She rattled off another dozen keywords that might be relevant. The computer began dinging, the alert stuttering with its sudden overload of information. "Computer: Mute. Run scan in background." She sighed in relief. Another few minutes and she set a scan to find local security and traffic cameras. Tomorrow she would see about accessing the data the government pulled from smart phones and computer webcams.

"Hey, Dan?"

He glanced back and tugged his earbuds out. "Yeah?"

"Do we have anyone in the Institute's payroll down there? People who keep an eye on the site?"

"Maybe a few. I can grab you a list of locals we've worked with before once I'm done here. Why, what's up?"

"Camera coverage is spotty. I want eyes on the local head of the Founders. Bently too, if we can spare them. Anyone who's not going to look suspicious in the area."

"Gotcha."

The computer dinged and she opened the update.

FLIGHT 273 CANCUN TO SANTIAGO DISEMBARKING NOW.

She tapped the screen, remembering a moment later to use the mouse. The airport's cameras bloomed into life, washed out, but clear. A few students traipsed out of the gate followed by a broad, tan-skinned man with dark brown hair. She glanced at the personnel files again. *Her site supervisor, Dr. Michael Servais.* And then Dr. Bently strode out, a battered bag over one shoulder. Lin made the feed full-screen. Dark blonde hair hung in shaggy layers around her shoulders, tucked back to show dark eyes. A loose t-shirt with the name of some archaeology firm showed strong shoulders. *She's pretty,* Lin realized, with some surprise. And she had Dar's determined, take-no-prisoner's stride. Lin leaned forward, peering at the screen until the group disappeared into customs.

"Are you ready for what you're about to find down there, Bently?"

CHAPTER FOUR

Lin flicked on the recordings of the crew's voices. It was close to midnight, but she still could not sleep. She had been dirt-side, as Dar often called it, for almost two weeks. *And nothing.* This was worse than any tedious project she had ever done in school. She always thought of the *Promise* as silent, at least compared to the constant rumble of the *Odyssey.* Now, faced with actual silence in the absence of space flight, she realized her body was accustomed to white noise. Dan's choice of podcasts and music was distracting at the best of times, but something in the voices of her subjects comforted her. *Mostly just Bently's.*

It was gravel, sharp and low in Lin's ears. She set the computer to scan the audio in case she fell asleep mid-listen, and turned off all recording but Dr. Bently's. There was little to record. Half the crew brought cheap phones for international plans, Bently included. They were harder to tap, since the lines weren't already under basic government surveillance. The archaeologist was complaining about the most recent case of Founder-related harassment. Apparently someone had followed Bently home, leaving footprints around the outside of the hotel the night before.

Lin curled into her pillows and brought up the profile she had made on the Founder's local leader. The low green glow hurt her eyes less than the bright blue of the computers in the lab. From what she had heard he was not a violent man. Calculating, perhaps, but not rash. The local police deputy the Institute used as an informant marked him as low-risk. A local bartender in the small town where Bently stayed thought Emilio's "local wise man" persona was entirely fabricated, but assumed it was for the tourists. Satisfied, she opened Bently's profile. It was updated with a photograph from one of the woman's reports. The few weeks in the sun since her arrival in Chile had brought a rich tan and scattered freckles to her cheeks. Her eyes were bright with the effects of whatever dark drink was gripped in her scarred hand.

A forgotten sensation tugged at Lin's gut. *I wish I could meet you.* They had all but forbidden her from going into the field on this mission.

Bently sounded angry, her words punctuated by the *pop-hiss* of a beer opening. "I just don't know. This is getting serious. I'm worried—and not just about the site. We have kids here and I don't want something to happen. Even the smallest issue could escalate when you have people who aren't prepared for this."

"We have plenty of legal legs to stand on." The low, drawling voice was that of Dr. Servais. Lin had gathered they were friendly, for coworkers. "But I get you. Do you think help would be good?"

"Oh, maybe. It's a little late in the game for that, though." The conversation lapsed, the quiet sounds of drinking and what might have been pages turning the only evidence that the connection was still active.

Lin frowned. If they thought they needed help, she should look into getting it for them. Her communication with Bently's department head had been sparse, just enough to introduce herself as an intern helping with the paperwork end of things for her own dissertation. It was close enough to the truth. She skimmed the list of the half a dozen archaeologists the Institute had already vetted if additional expertise was necessary. *Bently, you're good, but you can't be in two places at once.* The second file was a young man with black hair and kind eyes. A blue dot beside his name told her he had contracted or consulted with the Institute before. She opened an email correspondence.

To Dr. Martin de Santos of UNE

Thank you for your prompt response the other day regarding the vandalism. I am pleased with the level of professionalism and care the crew is taking. I would feel more comfortable if another PhD level archaeologist was present—not to take over for Drs. Bently and Servais, of course, but to aid them while they are under such stress. I would recommend Dr. Chad DiGregorio, as we're familiar with his work, but of course the ultimate choice is yours.

Thank you so much for your time, and I hope you are well.

Lin Nalawangsa

Intern, IDH

All the fatigue from the monotony of the day had left her limbs at the stress in Bently's voice. Her gaze slid to the glove resting on her nightstand. *I'm supposed to protect them. And they need help.* She had yet to test the weapon, or even put it on.

Perhaps it was time she did.

She glanced at the clock by her bed. It was odd not to have the time constantly flickering in the back of her mind, streaming from the suit's computer. It was almost midnight, but she was willing to bet Dan was still up.

Sure enough she found him hunched over a mug of steaming coffee. He looked more annoyed than exhausted.

"Long night?"

He glanced up. "Huh? Oh, hey Lin. Yeah, a bit. Headquarters sent in a sample of the *Odyssey*. Something involving the Emissaries."

Lin had forgotten most Terrestrials—and apparently those who spent enough time around them—called the Amba "Emissaries." "I heard there was an issue with communication a while back. Their planet went dark?"

"I guess. So little trickles down to us on this rock. What's got you up?" He pointed at the sputtering machine on the counter. "Coffee's fresh. Such as it is."

"I'm set." As much as she was enjoying the flavors of Earth, she drew the line at the use of unregulated stimulants. *Though it does smell good.* "Where would I go to learn how to use a glove?"

"As in, the super-hero electro-power weapons you all favor?"

"Yeah." Lin rubbed a thumb across her palm. "I'm rather new to it. Just upgraded before touch-down."

"Well I'm mostly waiting for machines to beep. I'd love a distraction."

"You know how?"

"Used to be really good with them too." He levered himself out of the plastic chair and stretched. "I bet we could use the empty bay of the garage. Walls are thick enough. Nothing too fragile."

Lin eyed the seemingly inert piece of fabric in her hand. "Hopefully that's not necessary."

Dan snorted and tossed his lab coat aside before they headed down the hall to the far side of the complex. "Plan for the worst, hope for the best, eh?"

"I feel like that's all this mission is. And waiting."

"That's all life is, baby." Dan's humor only grew as the night wore on, it appeared. He palmed the garage bay open, marching Lin to the far side out of range of the Jeep and smaller buggies used to service the arrays. "Stand by the door and face me. The cement will absorb the shock better than the metal." He glanced over his shoulder at her as he pulled a permanent marker out. "Don't you dare put that thing on until I'm out of the line of fire." A few sweeps of the marker later and he had drawn a large, cartoon face with what looked like the Founder's symbol emblazoned across the forehead.

"That's cute."

"Unlike with Terrestrial firearms, emotions help." Dan stopped beside her, watching as she tugged the fabric over her hand.

"Aren't they going to be upset you drew all over the garage?"

Dan's dark brows rose. "You're about to shoot the wall. I think a little Sharpie won't be an issue."

Maybe I should have had the coffee. She checked the connection to the snug electrofiber. It was body-temperature, only slightly stiffer than her own skin. She stretched her hand out. The palm grew warm. "And I just think 'shoot?'"

"You command it, the way you do your suit, but there's a secondary set of confirmation phrases. Like a safety."

"Safety?"

"It's a term from 20th century terrestrial firearms. Used to help prevent the gun from shooting."

"Dead-man's switch."

"Kind of, yeah. If you don't respond with the appropriate phrase the glove won't fire. If you don't respond at all, it sends a ping to your suit to broadcast a 'mayday' alert in case you've been incapacitated or are held hostage." He stepped back behind the firing zone and pointed to the target. "With yours, accuracy isn't needed as much. It's a pretty basic rig."

"That's alright." She raised the glove, bracing her wrist with her bare hand. "I'm learning I'm a pretty basic woman." *Electro-bast: Fire. Confirm action: fire electro-bast.* She swallowed hard and leaned into the thought, her lips cradling the words. "Confirm: Fire."

The glove surged with heat, her suit humming to compensate her body from the sudden energy drain. Her palm tingled, itched, then burned. The beam exploded from her hand, wavering as her body shook. The light was somewhere between blue and too bright to see. The image seared itself into her retinas. She clenched her hand and the beam fizzled into the glove. She blinked, then blinked again. Behind the black-orange after-image were the smoke remains of the target. "Oh."

Dan snorted. Then his chuckle bloomed into a deep-throated laugh. "That's a word for it. How'd ya feel?"

"Nauseous. Mostly."

"Yeah it's an adjustment. Some take stabilizers or downers before they shoot, but mostly I find it messes with my reaction time when I'm actually in a fight."

"You get in fights often? Where you use a glove, at least?" She eyed the tech. He looked like the only physical altercations he was accustomed to were massages.

"Pretty regularly." He fished a glove out of his pocket and pulled it on. The disk at the palm was slightly different than that on hers. "We get break-ins all the time.

People wanting to steal whatever data they think we're hiding. Kids trying to see the UFOs. And of course the Founders trying to destroy our lives' work." He flexed his hand and narrowed his eyes on the target. A series of beams burst from his palm.

Her brows arched. "Don't you get cold?"

He shrugged. "I do now, but when you're in the heat of it—pardon the pun—your body's natural adrenaline compensates most of it. It's the after-effects you want to watch out for. You need to rehydrate and take your normal course of recovery serum. Out in the desert like here the tech pulls most of the heat from the air, rather than your body, like it would in space."

She thought the Terrestrials were savage. Violent. Fighting over a 13,000 year old disagreement like children over whose turn it was in a playscape. Dar was the hopeful one, the one who dreamed of the stars while Lin struggled to see whatever it was the Amba had in her ancestors. But the Founders shared those ancestors. The Institute was bred of the same stock. The same chaos and violence flowed in the red of their blood. *Maybe we aren't so different.* Lin raised her hand, eyes narrowed, shoulders braced. Her arm pulsed. The air cooled over her goosebumped skin.

"Confirm: Fire."

CHAPTER FIVE

"Lin! Check out what just came in!" Dan swiveled his chair around. He held a small cardboard box with several stickers labeling the side.

"Your newest decoration for your 'workspace?'" Lin asked, sarcasm caressing the question with air-quotes. His desk was covered in brightly colored vinyl figurines.

"I'll have you know they boost my morale and therefore my efficiency. Just because I was born in a monochrome space station doesn't mean I have to behave like I still live in one."

"I don't understand how you can work like that, is all. So what's the package?"

"From your Dr. Bently, actually."

Lin dropped her device on the uninteresting pile of papers and rushed to his desk. In the week since Dr. DiGregorio arrived on site there had been little Founder activity to monitor and Lin's days were more boredom than history-altering discoveries. "Can I see?"

"If you stop trying to contaminate it with your curry breath, yes."

Lin clamped a hand over her mouth. "Sorry! I'm just really enjoying the flavors. The *Promise* doesn't have the same resources to allow for creativity when it comes to food. It's one of the biggest things I miss about living on the *Odyssey*."

"I hear you, there." He pulled a double-bagged chunk of black dirt from the package. It came with a sheet of paper, haphazard handwriting filling in the blanks on the typewritten label. "Well this is weird."

"What is that, dirt from her excavations?"

"Pretty much. When they find features like fire pits they send samples of both the soil surrounding them and within the feature itself to compare and get C-14 dates. We're the fastest lab—for obvious reasons." He patted the sleek black machine on the table next to his desk. It was something clearly designed for both the cramped space and esthetics of one of their ships, not the dingy white of the Terrestrial lab. "This though, this looks weird."

"How so?" She leaned over his shoulder, trying to take shallow breaths through her nose.

"The color. The soils out there are mostly dark yellow-brown silty medium sand. It varies, sure, but at least on the 10 or 7.5 YR page of their soil color books. But the sheen in this has is unique." He washed the outside of the bag with a cleansing wipe and placed it in the drawer of the enclosed chem hood before slipping his hands in the gloves.

"When were you there last?"

"Hmm?" He questioned as he transferred a few small scoops onto a series of trays for various component tests.

"On the *Odyssey*."

"When I was 16. I was tired of waiting to enlighten this world. I wanted to do it myself. Now I mostly listen to the stars and act as a relay between the Institute and NASA, but I enjoy it. Plus we consult on fun projects like this."

Lin frowned. "Maybe it came from having parents who were highly involved with two departments in the Institute, but I guess I just always trusted they knew best."

"You mean 'we?'" He caught her eye in the reflection of the hood's glass. "You do that a lot—speak about the Institute like you're not actually a part of it."

"I guess so." She looked away. She didn't think it was important, but Dan was trained to see trends and point out what was coincidence and what was statistically significant. *Maybe there's something to it.* "So, what is this? Ash from a firepit?"

Dan grinned. "She's gonna hate it." He held up a vial to the light. "I won't know until all the test are run, obviously, but I'd bet good money that this comes back positive for hydrocarbons. Not to mention various biproducts of electromagnetic ignition."

"So, she's found it?" Lin's heart thundered in her chest. The results on that stratum would change Bently's life. *Change her world.* Knowing the effect the tiny bag of dirt would have was a powerful drug.

Dan tugged his hands from the gloves and tapped the label Dr. Bently had filled out. "It says it's a sample of an abnormal, unknown strat. I'm betting she just came down on our ancestors' living surface. She's not going to like it when I tell her it's covered in rocket fuel."

Lin stared at the lumps of black soil. Mixed in the grains of sand her ancestors walked upon tens of thousands of years ago, was humanity's future. Until Dr. Bently opened the lab results in a week, everyone could pretend it was a normal, prehistoric site. *One week before history is made. Again.* "Do you think they're ready?"

"I think they've been for a while. Part of me wonders if that's why everything seems more violent, closer, angrier. Maybe we waited too long."

"And you're going to give her the accurate results?"

"I mean, you control what information is given. But I was planning on it. What she does with it, that's a whole other story. She's a driven woman, but man, is she stubborn. Wouldn't have gotten so far without being that way."

"I wish I could meet her."

"I'm surprised you haven't already. You will, I'm sure, when this gets closer to publication."

Lin hummed in response, her mind already churning with the mental image Dan's description brought up. The woman in the academic profile looked driven. His words made her sound almost muleish. Lin wanted as much distance between herself and this desperate, rough world. *But I wouldn't mind meeting her.* "What do you think she could say, to write it off?"

"Contamination is always a possibility. Dates get wonky all the time from an impure sample. We don't like to admit it, but even with our tech there's a big margin of error. Not to mention, she's working with students, and she doesn't know how advanced our tech is." He patted the folder he tucked the file into. "Who knows, maybe you could hand-deliver her the results. An in-person invitation to a better world."

Goosebumps drifted over Lin's arms at the thought. "I think I'd like that. She seems fascinating."

Dan glanced at the profile, then up at Lin. "She's cool, for sure. I'll give you that." His eyes narrowed and Lin frowned.

"What?"

"I'm trying to decide if she's going to hate you, or fall in love with you."

Lin's cheeks flushed and she pushed the thought aside. Her relationship with Bently was built on a mountain of misinformation and they had yet to even meet. From what she knew already, the archaeologist was unforgiving. It did not bode well.

Her computer beeped, insistent and patient. Lin pulled up her computer's alert. "Uh oh." Intermittent signal and lack of good audio taps, it regularly took days before the computer scanned enough to know when something was suspicious. The video feeds were more reliable, but only slightly. The transcript was of a conversation a few nights before. It accompanied a video feed from the front of a restaurant run by Emilio Sepulveda, one of the local Founders. The video, though grainy, showed the entire crew out to dinner. Most were laughing, Nel seemed to be enjoying her third or fourth beer of the evening.

"Computer: Sync audio feed with video timestamp, please."

"Why do you do that? Say 'please,' like it cares?"

She hadn't realized she did. It reminded her of Phil and she fought a wave of homesickness. "I think because of Phil. You guys ever use senti-comps?"

"Centipedes, what?" Dan turned with a frown, microscopic goggle still hung over the lens of his lab glasses.

Lin giggled. "Senti-comps. The sentient ship computers we use."

"Oh, right. Last time I was on board they were just referred to as managers. Never use them here. I think they make most Terrestrial folk nervous. They make me nervous. Too much about where they came from is unclear. Never even seen one in person."

"A few years ago they started referring to themselves differently. I miss it, the background voice. Always someone to talk to. *Promise* is managed by Phil. Philos."

Dan shuddered. "I guess I'm just not ready to give up the illusion of privacy yet." He glanced at the half-dozen camera feeds on Lin's computer screen. "Even if it is just an illusion."

She snorted and turned back to the screen to listen. Someone was telling a story about goats on a site. Food and plates clattered. Bently swore. *Nothing new there,* Lin thought with a grin. She frowned, cranking the audio. *There.* The words that pinged the scan: "Bad publicity and some vandalism I can deal with, though it never makes me happy. I feel like I have to watch my back every second." Bently continued, then Emilio himself appeared. Lin's brows rose. It seemed the archaeologists had no idea of his connection with their antagonists.

Though it wasn't clear, what she gathered from the student's audio was someone had put something in Bently's food—something dead. Lin's body went cold. That was a direct threat. It could have hurt her. *How do I know when it's time to go in? How do I tell the difference between "far" and "too far" when I don't even know the details?*

Her reports to Dr. Ndebele's team and Dar were met with "let us know when something changes" response, often verbatim to the previous one. She wasn't willing to admit her concern to Dr. Ndebele herself, yet. Dar, on the other hand, would at least steer her in the right direction. *With no small amount of condescension.* They might not have been close, but there was still loyalty. She watched as the crew left the restaurant, then paused the feed. "I'll be right back. I need to make a call."

"Roof's got good signal if you need privacy." Dan offered, eyes glued, once again, to the pile of dark, glimmering dirt.

Lin tucked her com into her pocket and jogged down the hall. The building was the hulking square block that

most industrial science facilities favored. Lin preferred
the stark elegance of the *Odyssey's* labs, but she was
quickly learning Earth's labs spoke of a world that did not
value science as much as other pursuits.

She shoved open the heavy door to the rooftop and
let the wind buffet her. Wind was a wonder against her
skin. The vacuum of space, the rush of recycled air—even
the clean breath of the forest that powered the *Odyssey*—
nothing compared to the blast of dry wind carrying the
scent of sand and burning soil. *Maybe that's why Dan
loves it here. Everything is immediate, intense,
unavoidable.* She wondered if it would grow on her, as
well, if she were here longer than the few weeks allotted
for the mission. Already her view on the Terrestrial
humans changed from polite disinterest to curiosity. She
recognized the stubbornness in Bently's voice from her
own, from Dar's, from her mother's.

She tilted her face to the sun for a moment. Earth was
the only place she could feel the sun on her skin without
layers of glass and steel. Only a thin lens of molecules
curled protectively between her and burning, freezing
oblivion.

She opened her com and dialed up to the *Promise.*
"Phil, this is Letnan First Class Lin Nalawangsa, to speak
to Komodor Muda Udara Dar Nalawangsa. Unofficial
com, please."

"Connecting." There was a pause. "How is it, down
there?"

She had never known the computer to be curious. "Windy." It was the first thing she thought of. "Everything is closer, I guess."

"I remember wind."

Lin frowned. "You've been here?"

"I'm from there. Connected." The line clicked and Dar's voice replaced Phil's.

"Lin?"

"Evening, Dar."

"Morning, actually."

I didn't realize I'd forget so easily. "Morning, then. How is the *Promise?*"

"Same as ever. Our mission is moving forward."

"What's that?" She had been bundled off-ship too quickly to ask what mission took them so far from home.

"A terrestrial country we allied with just claimed to prefer the Founders. They call themselves 'Deep Roots' there. We enter negotiations in two days."

"The Founders are my issue, as well." She could picture the almost robotic change in focus on his face. There were times he seemed as computerized as Phil. There were times he seemed more.

"I think I need to go in. They've been vandalizing the site for weeks."

"Lin, I know Dr. Ndebele said you could monitor from a closer vantage, but I don't feel that you're capable of handling the situations that might arise. If anything, the archaeologists might be better suited to dealing with vandalism. They've had to in the past."

"I think this is different," Lin argued. "And if you all felt that way then why am I here?"

"The Founders range from mild hazing and piss in water systems to lighting buildings they know contain our servers on fire. Where exactly on that spectrum did they fall this time?" He seemed unwilling to answer her question.

"They put something dead or toxic in Nel's food. Wherever that is, on your spectrum."

"Nel?"

"Dr. Bently."

Dar faded into silence for a moment. She could hear the hum of the distance between them, a faint series of beeps and whirs as he paced from one end of his room to another. "No direct violence?"

"Putting something in food is violent to me, but no, no direct violence. Some lurking on hill tops. Meaningful, angry eye-contact. I heard Dr. Bently talking to her crew chief about some photo on a website. I gather they didn't think it was serious enough, since it didn't show up anywhere in their text communication later."

"Or they were threatened. Did you run their voices through Emotion?"

Lin winced. It was something she should have thought of. Something she was trained to think of. She had grown so used to listening to their voices that part of her wondered if she would know better than a computer. "I can do that now. I didn't hear anything that made me think deeper analysis was necessary."

"Deeper analysis is always necessary. Don't go in. Do your job there, do it better. If you still think it's necessary, then we'll talk."

The hard tone in his voice made her skin crawl.

"Who is the field director for this mission, Dar?"

"Excuse me?" He sounded more surprised than angry, but she was clearly circling dangerous territory.

"You heard me. You're not the field director here. I am. It's my job to know these people, and know what is significant for them. I promise, she's always like that. If I ran a recording of Dr. Bently's voice during orgasm, it would still sound angry. If you want me to analyze the situation, then let me. Let me go in. Let me talk to her, review the site, see the artifacts. I can do a lot from here, but I can do the most important part—protect them."

"Lin, I told you, stick to the mission guide unless something extremely out of the ordinary comes up. And then I would argue let us handle it. You're monitoring, not helping."

This is out of the ordinary, even if you can't be bothered to care. Lin bit back the nasty comment. "Fine, but if that's the case I'm going on record right now and saying I think I need to go in. I think it's dangerous not to have as much information as we can."

"Recorded. Now go watch your screens and please call me if something happens."

"I will." She clicked off without goodbye and tugged the com from her ear. Her hands shook with checked frustration. Perhaps they were right that she didn't need to meet Nel herself, but she still wanted to help. *And Dar wouldn't know what help looked like if it crawled down his throat and shook hands with his appendix.*

CHAPTER SIX

"I don't know why this is so important to them. To any of us, really." Lin slumped at the round table in the kitchen. She had not sent a report to the *Promise* since she spoke to Dar almost a week ago. A quiet rebellion. *A useless rebellion.*

"It's where we're from." Dan offered. His tone told her he knew she was being stubborn.

She pursed her lips. She did get it. It was their history. As much as she felt her people and terrestrial humans were far from the same, the tug of genetics was there. But she had never felt so alien, and it flipped her world on its head. "We're from *Odyssey*. Even if you refuse to acknowledge it."

His morning-bleary eyes were fixed on a faded map of the world pinned to the wall beside a bulletin board of workers' safety fliers. If his gaze wasn't inching over every border and mountain range she would have assumed he was lost in thought. "All of us, I mean." His brows curled together for a fleeting moment, as if he looked on something sacred. She supposed, for him, it might be.

A poorly scaled image depicting the relative size of all the planets in their solar system was pinned on the other side of the board, each sphere squeezed beside the next. Earth was a blue-green pea tucked into the foreground. She wondered for a moment where the *Odyssey* would fit on the scale.

Shrill beeping interrupted whatever sanctity the moment held. Lin peered at her wrist com.

"Bently?"

"No, it's Emilio Sepulveda." She shoved herself to her feet. "Sounds like an argument." As much as she hated the stillness of surveillance, she enjoyed the puzzle. Each recording of audio or scanned digital communication was a piece of a puzzle, an image forming in real time.

The computers hummed into glowing wakefulness. *Why is the computer picking up fear?* She double checked the read out. Her wrist-com hadn't been wrong. The readings were for the head of The Founders, and fear was high.

She pressed the headphones over her ears and turned up the volume. It was inside, and a small room by the muffled sound. Emilio's rumbled Spanish came in clear through the tapped cell phone.

"You don't understand, Bastian. You can't stop them from discovering it—they already have. They've taken readings, they've found a body, for God's sake."

"If it's too late why did you bother to threaten them on the road? You're getting more cowardly by the day, Sepulveda." The second voice was the scrape of gravel, a bitter tone that belonged to Bastian, Emilio's second-in-command.

Threaten? Lin scanned the files from the past week, but nothing came up. At Dar's request, she had run their voices through Emotion for the past week. Stress levels were high, and lights flickered for each subset of anger, exhaustion, excitement. *But never fear.*

Even when Nel called about the results Dan sent her, her voice never wavered into anything but frustration.

"Bas, stand down. We did not make it this far with rash decisions and guns. That's the Institute's job. We protect our history. We protect these people from making the same mistake the ancestors of IDH did thousands of years ago."

"We can't trust them, not with how global everything has become. This data gets out and the world knows within days. Hours, even." Bastian's voice pitched from frustration to anger, then settled into resolve. Worry bloomed in Lin's gut. *Resolve to do what?*

"You go in waving a gun again and you'll attract attention. People are fascinated by secrets, and if they know you're terrified of them discovering this one, they'll wonder why."

"You're a damned coward, Sepulveda. If you won't handle this, I will." A door slammed, followed by stillness.

Lin pressed the headphones over her ears. Emilio sighed, and she caught the sound of shuffling papers. "Sometimes," he murmured, as if he spoke in her ear, a confession just for her, "sometimes I wonder which side is right. Sometimes I think neither is, anymore."

"Emilio?" She couldn't help the word the slipped from her mouth. Surveillance bred a strange, insidious intimacy.

"What was it?" Dan's voice pierced the quiet, startling a yelp from her. "Sorry, I didn't mean to scare you."

She shoved the headphones away and gripped her head in her hands. "I don't know what to do, Dan." She was tired of watching through the grainy pixels of security cameras, through the crackling connection of rural phone lines.

His dark eyes narrowed on her. "I think you do know. You just don't know if you should."

She stared at the academic photo that accompanied Nel's bio for a moment. "How long does it take to get to the site?"

"Six hours, maybe more if traffic is bad through Antofagasta. It's a pretty straight shot though." His hand hovered over the phone. "I can get a car called up if you want."

Six hours. I'd arrive when they got out of work. She would look over the site, make sure everything was safe, then head back. She could be back by midnight. Dar would be furious. Dr. Ndebele would be disappointed. *But Nel and her crew will be safe.* "Call a car, please. I'm leaving in fifteen."

Dan grinned. "See, breaking the mold is fun. Next you'll be telling me you're moving to Earth."

She snorted. "I'll set the system to beep if something suspicious happens. My com should pick it up, but signal is awful there, even with the extra satellites. Text if it goes off, will you?"

"Will do. How long you think you'll be gone?"

She shrugged. "Not long. 1 AM at the latest. I'll get on the com if something comes up."

"You better. I'm not answering to either Komodors Nalawangsa, Muda or otherwise." He swiveled his seat back to his work. "Be careful."

"I will." It took a minute to jog back to her bedroom. A trip to the commissary a few days before resulted in a few sets of terrestrial clothes. She pulled on the leggings and tee-shirt that were her favorite. They reminded her of the suits she was used to, close and flexible. She tucked her long-range com next to her borrowed mobile in the pocket on her thigh. A slim gray case held her glove and various forged documents claiming she was an intern for IDH. After a second's deliberation, she added a gray suit. *It wouldn't hurt to look official if I have to.*

She shoved through the ALMA front doors to find an old gray sedan waiting. Sand and dry air ripped through her hair, whipping it against her cheeks. She tucked herself into the back seat, heart pounding. They turned onto the road to Antofagasta and Lin pressed her forehead to the tinted glass of the window. After a minute, the signal to her com flickered into static.

CHAPTER SEVEN

The sun slung low when the driver pulled onto a battered paved road. Ahead a small town glittered between the hill's knees. Lin checked the map on her wrist com and tapped the glass between herself and the driver. "Right up here—you can leave me at the bottom of that road."

"Should I wait?" The driver asked, peering over her sunglasses through the rearview mirror.

"Please. I shouldn't be more than an hour or two." Lin promised, pulling on a thin sweatshirt.

"I'll be in town, just call."

She nodded and slipped from the car. Hard soil crunched underfoot. The sunbaked day had become a mild evening. A quick climb later, she was following the ridge along the road. It wound down through the hills towards the sea. *And beyond that is the site.* In spite of her pragmatic outlook, anticipation shivered up her arms. Her ancestors had walked these very hills thousands of years ago.

She was less than a kilometer away when she realized her glove was still tucked in its case in the backseat of the sedan. This time the shiver that crawled up her body had nothing to do with the breeze. *I shouldn't need it.* She barely knew how to use it. She had practiced twice since Dan's lesson, and it still felt unnatural on her hand. *"… rash decisions and guns. That's the Institute's job."* She took a breath. Perhaps they needed conversation. Diplomacy. Despite what her father's favorite terrestrial films said, Lin knew that even with a few space-ships, prehistoric archaeology very rarely involved shoot-outs and bloodshed.

She paused on the hilltop overlooking a sheltered dip in the landscape. It was dusk, not the proper dim light for such an exploration, but the shadows were long enough to hide in. Something dropped with a clatter below and she froze.

A peek past the rock told her Bently left someone behind. The man below wrestled with the sullen yellow lump of the total station. His mutters were more puzzled than frustrated and half in French, the other in English. *Michael Servais, Crew Chief.* Finally, he unbolted the thing from its stand and settled it into the open case at his feet.

Then the first gunshot went off. Lin ducked, as much from surprise as instinct. When she looked up, three men were stalking from the road toward him.

"Sonuva bitch!" Servais's voice cracked with surprise. His hands, high above his head, shook. "Christ, guys." He switched to Spanish. "I get it. You don't want us here. We're not disrespecting your heritage. We have permission from every recognized native organization. You're way out of bounds here! Let's get the cops up here and we can chat it out like sane folk, OK?"

Lin's heart thundered. *Bastian.* She only recognized one other man, but Emilio was not among them. A crowbar thwacked against Servais's knee. The second man's fist caught Servais's chin as he fell. The third's boot cracked ribs.

Acid crawled up Lin's throat and she pressed herself into the ground. Her hand inched to the edge of the rise, just far enough that the com might capture what she couldn't face. The blows went from *thwacks* to *thuds*, to quiet, wet sounds. Dirt puffed from her silent gasps. *The Founders? This makes no sense.* Emilio Sepulveda wasn't that kind of man. She may not have met a single person in those personnel files, but she memorized their behavior, their personalities. *Bastian is mutinying.*

"I thought we weren't killing them?"

"I thought you were in this for keeps. Besides, someone was setting off our scans—someone here has tech that isn't local."

"Bas—"

"Don't use my fucking name. This whole place could be hot for all we know."

She frowned. It was a voice she couldn't place, but she tucked it away for later. *Please don't search the place.*

"Shouldn't we take a look around?"

"No, go get the car. I'm going over the rise to the river, see if they've found the door yet. Pick me up on the road when you have the body loaded."

Door? Lin listened to the crunch of bootfalls fading up the road. When it had been silent for a minute she surged to her feet. The site below was deserted, save for the assistant crew chief. She skittered down the slope, wincing at every sharp clack of rocks sliding in her wake. Coarse sand bit into her knees as she knelt. His face was a bloody mess of knotted tissue and broken zygomatics. One eye was swollen shut, the other flooded with blood. Pulsing blood from his ruined forearm was the only sign of life.

"Dr. Servais?"

He groaned, spitting blood. "Who's there?"

"I'm Lin, I'm from—nevermind, we don't have time. I'll help you." She gripped the shoulders of his shirt and pulled. He wasn't light, but she was strong, made stronger from years of gravity training. They were almost at the edge of the site when she heard the rumble of a truck barreling up the road. "They're coming!" *I can't leave him.* She dragged him another few meters. Each tug drew a groan from his split lips. The truck slid to a halt, dust billowing from the churning tires. Two men jumped out. One raised a gun in his shaking hand. Lin surged upright, planting her feet on either side of Servais's body. "You can't have him!"

"Who the fuck are you?"

Adrenaline burst through her veins and she snarled. "We're the people your fathers warned you about. And you can't stop us." She raised her hand and thought, *Fire.*

Her hand was empty.

Oh no. Broken fingers gripped her ankle. She glanced down. Servais's hand trailed blood across her leggings. He muttered something. "What?"

"Go!" The word was spat with blood and teeth and dying breath.

She glanced at the two men, still uncertain, waiting for fire or lightning to shoot from her bare palm. Then she was running. She didn't stop at the rise, or when the gun finally barked behind her. Her legs churned, carrying her over the rocky hills and down towards the coast. The man's words rang in her head like the echo of gunfire. *Tech that isn't local.* She glanced down at the com still gripped in her right hand. *They thought it was Servais.* She chewed back guilt and slowed to a jog. The desert was dark, but cool and her thighs burned, even in the lower gravity. In every report she promised Dar it was under control. *And Ayah trusted me.* But now someone was dead.

And she had left him behind.

CHAPTER EIGHT

Lin was grateful her driver was not a conversationalist. The long drive back to ALMA was silent, save for the tap of her exhausted fingers on her phone as she drafted her resignation. She knew there was no way she could return to the *Promise,* when her actions had gotten someone killed. How could she guide Nel's discovery with this secret yawning between them? *I've got to make this right.*

She paused her typing and brought up the search engine.

Annelise Bently archaeology.

A series of web pages popped up, mostly academic papers or references to various research programs. For someone in their mid-thirties she was prolific. The fifth search result was a social media page. The picture was a far cry from Bently's academic photo.

The woman had a broad, crooked grin. Her dark blonde hair was shoulder-length still, but in disarray. One hand clenched a beer that was in danger of spilling Her other arm was flung over the shoulder of a young man. Lin's stomach lurched. It was the man she just watched die. His skin was light brown, his curls collected in short dreadlocks. He wasn't looking at the camera. He stared at Bently with more brotherly love than Dar ever showed her.

"Oh no." She thought he was her site supervisor. She thought he was her colleague. *They're best friends.*

The car eased to a halt. She shoved the door open to see Dan waiting for her at ALMA's broad glass doors.

"Hey." Her words rattled over the gravel of exhaustion and emotion in her throat.

"You look like hell." He waved away his own words, steering her down the hall to the same kitchenette where their morning had begun. It seemed like centuries had passed since then. He flopped into the chair across from her and offered a vial of stimulant. "What happened?"

She took it, but couldn't bring herself to put it in her port. *I deserve to feel terrible.* She didn't know where to begin. Her hands shook. She suddenly wished she was wearing her suit so something, even if it was just electro fiber, could hold her. Instead her skin was too weak to contain the flood of words. "Someone's dead, Dan, and I'm scared."

"Who's dead? A Founder?"

"No. One of the crew." The words broke the shell keeping her emotions at a manageable level. Her voice shuddered through her teeth. "I went to see what the site looked like, how close they were to where we thought the site would be. Maps don't do it justice. Dr. Bently's second in command, Servais, was there, trying to fix their survey equipment it looked like."

"Yeah they've been having trouble, probably due to the residual magnetism. Did he attack you?"

"No, no, nothing like that he was—" Tears spilled over her cheeks. It had been years since she cried. "I'm not used to so many feelings, everything being so close, so quick, so immediate." She drew a breath and tried to steady herself. "Some of the Founders showed up. I guess they have some access to a scan that picks up any non-terrestrial tech. They thought it was him, that he was setting it off. It was me. They beat him close to death and I couldn't stop it. I tried, but—"

Dan touched her hand. "If you need to tell me, you can, but I can just look at the video feed."

Lin passed him her com. "Please." She closed her eyes when he pressed play, listening to the sound of tires, Servais's voice, the blows, the scraping as she pulled his body along. Finally the gunshot. "The shot, was it me or…?"

"It was Servais." His voice had changed. There was sorrow, but also frustration. "You didn't bring your glove?"

"I forgot it in the car. I barely know how to use the thing. I was trained, once, years ago, on an older model. I'd be so worried about how to use it I'd probably blow myself up somehow. I wish I knew, I wish I had thought to bring it."

"It looks like your instinct took over there." He dipped his head to catch her downcast eyes. "Touching down in strange. The emotions, and the desperation of having this place be it, they're the strangest thing you realize when you get here. This world is immediate. Up there, it takes years to get anywhere. Everything has a planned trajectory, a mission statement. If you get too concerned or sad or worried then you can pop something in your port and within a minute realize that everything is going to be fine. Everything is always going to be fine. Down here, we're all there is. Very little is ever fine. But honestly? It makes everything we do mean more."

"I don't know how you stand it."

His smile was sad. "It's really easy to say they're too angry, too violent, too obsessed with base needs, when you don't realize the context, eh?"

"Really." She finally popped the vial into her arm and took a steadying breath. "I'm sure Dar is going to pull me out of this at any minute."

"Have you called them? Or your parents?"

"I don't know what to say."

"I think start with 'I'm OK' and go from there." He shoved himself to his feet. "Are you? OK that is?"

"I think so. She flashed him a smile she did not feel and wished him a good night. When the kitchenette was deserted once more, she brought up her father's number and requested the connection. After talking to Phil and then the senti-comp of her father's ship, the line crackled into life.

"Nalawangsa. Go."

"Hey Ayah." She couldn't keep the hurt from her voice, keep the tremble from her words.

"What's going on? Are you alright? Does this have to do with the message from your brother asking if I'd heard from you?"

"Probably, yeah." She drew a shuddering breath. "One of the crew members died. Someone I was supposed to protect. And it's my fault, or at least, indirectly. He was Dr. Bently's friend. Dar's right, they aren't ready for this, for us. I'm not ready." Her breath waved through her clenched teeth. She remembered his words before she touched down weeks ago. "I think I need to hear that story now."

"Oh, Dewdrop." She heard a door shut, muffling the chatter of the Navigation deck. That was a father's love—silencing the entire command center of a space ship because his daughter was crying. "When you were little you wanted, more than anything, to fly in a EVA pod. Suit up, tootle around the space station, the whole deal. I was horrified. I didn't want you leaving the station in a battle cruiser, let alone a tiny pod. I flatly forbade you to go."

"I remember. I cried for days. I thought I'd never get to explore."

"Right. Then I caught you in a Level 5 suit—backwards, I might add—loading up the access for the EVA. That was when your mother sat me down. She told me that you were going to do what you wanted, whether I approved or not. She said my job wasn't to stop you from doing dangerous things. It was to give you all the tools to do them well and as safely as possible."

Her heart ached at the memories. She missed family. She missed the station. She remembered the weightlessness, the blackness of space swallowing the EVA pod as they drifted farther from the station, her father's gloved hands over her tiny ones on the nav-stick. The adrenaline that shot through her body when he let go. "You seemed excited."

"I was terrified. You could have hurt yourself. There were dozens of things you did and you scraped your knee or cut yourself. But you did them. A human life is big. But sometimes lives are lost in exploration. In awakening. In learning. Don't make him die for nothing. It doesn't matter if we think they're ready. Someone does. They do, even if they don't know what it is yet. They're going to fall. And at some point they are going to have to catch themselves."

"Dar's not going to like this."

"You're mission head, Lin. Not him."

"I got demoted."

"You got transferred. He's your ship's officer, but not your commanding officer. I think you need to sit with this, try and sleep, and approach it again in the morning. I trust you."

"Da, I'm scared."

"Good. Now do something about it."

She was certain she would resign an hour ago. Now the drive that brought her to Earth, that kept her awake listening to the crew's voices, returned. "Thank you." She tapped "end call" and sat back. *Lives are lost in exploration. It's regrettable, but those people died for something they believed in. So make it worthwhile.* She pulled up the message. "Computer: Send Message to Komodor Muda Udara Dar Nalawangsa." She waited for the chime indicated the computer was ready for her dictation. "Dar, I've thought about our conversation. I've decided to move forward. I believe humans are ready for us, whether we think they are or not. They're reaching for the stars. It's about time we gave them a boost. I'll report when I know more. Computer: End message."

"Reply needed?"

"No. Open website for Institute for the Development of Humanity. Employee access page. Mission control for Mission: Hometown. Open all forms and files and permits that were suspended in the last week." The folders opened, a flicker of brighter light across the screen. "Funding for Archaeological Excavation of Los Cerros Esperando VII. Status: Reactivate. Permits for Archaeological Excavation of Los Cerros Esperando VII. Status: Reactivate." She moved through every file, the bold words changing in a green wave across her screen.

She needed to update her passport and buy a suit, but in a few days she would be Intern Lin Nalawangsa, arriving from Santiago to handle the legal nightmare Nel faced. Now she just had to memorize every lie she was about to tell.

CHAPTER NINE

The scent of alcohol and hand-rolled cigarettes seared Lin's nose. The bar door slammed behind her as she stifled a sneeze. *They spend all their energy trying to be immortal, and all their free time trying to kill themselves faster.* She caught herself. "We. Ourselves." It wouldn't due to be caught this early in the game.

"Buenos dias, senorita." The bartender folded his wiry arms across the wooden bar. "I'm Jerod, what can I do for you?"

She smiled and slipped into Spanish. "Excuse me, I'm looking for the Vecuna y Las Rosas." She knew where the hotel was, but she also knew this bar was one of Nel's haunts.

Jerod shrugged and shook his head with a cough. "They're all booked out, but there's an inn on the other side of town." His welcome had faded into a guarded, evaluating stare.

Lin perched on a barstool, setting her case beside her. The fact that some of the locals still seemed friendly, if not loyal, to Dr. Bently, gave Lin a spark of hope. "I'm looking for a woman staying there, actually. Annelise Bently. I'm from Santiago."

The bartender forced a laugh. "You're sure not from around here. It's down the road a ways. Turn left at the red three-story." He stopped, as if expecting her to turn right back around and leave. "Not sure if she's in. If I see her, who should I say was asking?" he lead.

Lin's brows rose at that. It was still morning. She hadn't known many Terrestrials to drink before noon. *She just lost someone.* "You think you're likely to see her in a bar at ten in the morning?" She waved away the man's continued silence and offered her name and hand.

"What did you just say?" The music from the jukebox in the corner ground to a swift halt. The person leaning on it turned, unsteady. It was a woman, dressed for outdoors. Her skin was tan under the sheen of sweat and dusting of dirt. She stumbled against one of the seats and belched.

Lin sighed. As much as she wanted to learn about Bently, drunk tourists would be little help. She slid into her best haughty Dar impression. "Excuse me?"

"Who'd you say you were?"

"It's not important." Lin thanked the bartender and grabbed her case. Her hand was on the crooked screen door when the drunk managed to sputter out half a dozen intelligible words.

"It's me. I'm Nel. Los Cerros Esperando VII, the site, it's mine."

Confusion curled around Lin's thoughts. Dr. Bently was driven, smart, and tough. Nothing scared her. Nothing shook her. *She's not a bloodshot-eyed drunk.*

The woman staggered over to the bar and ordered another drink. Under the dirt and sheen of sweat, Lin supposed the woman might have been tan. Her hair, though darkened from lack of bathing, was the right shade. Lin missed the comment Bently shot at her, but whatever the words, the tone was snide.

"I see." Lin steeled her nerves. Nel would be a bigger challenge than she realized, but that alone ignited her blood with curiosity.

Jerod slid a drink over to the archaeologist and raised his brows at Lin.

"Scotch." With her drink in hand, she turned to Nel. The woman was staring. Under the buzzing naked bulbs of the bar, Lin saw the other woman's brown eyes were as battered from a barrage of tears as from alcohol.

"Why are you here?" Bently scratched her throat, the motion distracted. "We got shut down. No need for you to get your hands dirty. Could have pulled our funding with a nice long 'fuck-you,'" she waved her hands in an exaggeration of signing something, "on company letterhead."

"Ms. Bently I didn't come to pull your funding." She glared at her drink in an effort to keep from rolling her eyes as Bently slurred her way into a tirade about being called "miss."

"…Third of all, you'll talk plainly, or I'm walking out." Bently swiveled her head back down to the bar. "I'd make you walk out. I'm not done drinking yet."

Of course you're not. Because why would this be easy. "We heard about the accident and I came to help.

We're not pulling funding. I'm filing paperwork to reopen your site."

The woman just finished her drink and thanked the bartender. She looked ready to weep again. When Lin prompted her for a response, Bently glared. "You want me to thank you, kiss your fucking Jimmy Choos? You show up late, waving your fucking shiny business card. I'm not going to thank you. My site is shut down. My site manager—" She trailed off in a rattle of words, then found her verbal footing again. "It wasn't a fucking accident and the guys who did it have been vandalizing our stuff all season. I've got shit to do, woman, and none of it involves you."

Frustration bloomed in Lin's gut. Grief was fine. This was ironclad stubbornness. If she couldn't convince the woman to work with her, the mission was as good as over. "I get that you have a lot to deal with. So would you care to tell me why you're drunk at ten in the morning?"

Nel snarled and tottered to her feet. She stalked from the bar, slamming the door behind her. Lin turned back to her drink. Alcohol was rarely permitted anywhere but the largest of ships or the space station. It was a drain on resources better used for transporting water. When it burnt its way down her throat, though, she understood the draw. *Rebirth by fire.*

"Will that be all, Miss?"

She glanced at the bartender. "Yes. I apologize for driving away your clientele."

He waved his hand at her. "She'll be back. There's only so often I can listen to the same song. I just don't have the heart to ask her to stop."

"No, I suppose not."

He seemed locked in an internal debate, his eyes narrowed on her, fingers drumming a tattoo on the worn bar. "Where did you say you were from, again?"

Lin turned her focus to him. "Excuse me?"

"I was told someone might come looking for Bently, there. And I was given a message for that person. What organization do you work for?"

"The Institute for the Development of Humanity. It's a philanthropic group with some wealthy patrons is all. Dr. Bently was lucky enough to catch our attention."

Jerod's slight smile did not reach his eyes. "I know who you are. Who the Institute is. What it is. I'll give you information, but I did my own digging." He reached under the bar.

Lin thrust her hand in her pocket, fumbling to straighten out the glove's fingers.

"Easy there, Miss." Jerod raised his unarmed hands. "I'm just getting a letter." He handed over the envelope. "When you're done you'd best be on your way. I'm sure Bently could use a hand stumbling back."

Lin knew a dismissal when she heard one. "I'll be just a moment." She tugged the letter free and unfolded it. It was handwritten and short:

To whomever cleans up this mess

I want you to know I never intended death to come here again. It brings with it an ugly shadow that lingers. I do not agree with you, but nor do I think my forefathers were entirely right. I hope while you are here we could find some time to talk. This may have begun with violence but it doesn't have to end that way.

You can find me at Padritos

-Emilio Sepulveda, Los Pobladores.

Lin ran a hand over the letter. It wasn't what she expected, but then again, none of this mission had been. She tucked it in her briefcase and finished her drink. "Thank you, Jerod." She rose, "Bueanos dias." She slipped from the bar and made her way back through town. The air was hot already, and a faint haze softened the edges of the buildings. A grin slid over Lin's mouth. She pulled up the file she wrote in the small hours of the morning after Servais's death. She changed a few lines, then tapped her com. "Send File: Resignation to Komodor Muda Udara Dar Nalawangsa."

She clicked off then tucked away the com. If she was going to talk to Nel, it would be woman-to-woman. Human-to-human.

Down the road, Nel's unsteady stomps released puffs of dirt from the packed earth. The archaeologist stopped for a moment and turned back, her bleary glare finding Lin's face. The fire in her expression sparked adrenaline, inspiration in Lin's chest.

The stars were Dar's mystery, his inspiration. She had explored the stars. It may have been where they were all headed, together, but the stars were a mystery she was willing to live with. The eight billion people clawing, clamoring to exist on this whirling rock were different. Her black gaze traced the dry boot prints of the archaeologist storming, drunk through the tiny Chilean town.

The stars aren't the final frontier. People are.

AMPHIBIAN ANTHOLOGIES

Out of the Darkness (Fantasy)

Beamed Up (Science Fiction)

Surrender to Passion (Romance)

My Soul To Take (Ghost Stories/Hauntings)

Crossbones (Pirates)

Switching Gears (Steampunk)

Dudes in Distress (Romance)

www.ingramcontent.com/pod-product-compliance
Lightning Source LLC
Chambersburg PA
CBHW031237120726
47905CB00002B/625